They Called Her Eve...

The snake woman grabbed him, wrapping her body around his, her lips seeking his mouth. Raider kissed her for a long time, but he kept thinking of the python behind them. He broke away finally.

"Don't you want me?" she asked, running her hands down to his crotch.

Raider gestured back toward the cage. "Ole Lucifer there has got me spooked."

"Oh, he won't eat you alive. But maybe I will."

He had to admit that she was appealing. But the damned snake was watching.

RAIDER

SIXGUN CIRCUS

J.D. HARDIN

BERKLEY BOOKS, NEW YORK

SIXGUN CIRCUS

A Berkley Book/published by arrangement with
the author

PRINTING HISTORY
Berkley edition/August 1987

ISBN: 0-425-10115-0

A BERKLEY BOOK ® TM 757,375
Berkley Books are published by the Berkley Publishing Group,
200 Madison Avenue, New York, NY 10016
The name "BERKLEY" and the "B" logo
are trademarks belonging to the Berkley Publishing Corporation

PRINTED IN THE UNITED STATES OF AMERICA

10 9 8 7 6 5 4 3 2 1

Dedicated to S.W.S. and J.O.C.

And to Peter McEvoy

PROLOGUE

"Raider, honey, don't go. Please stay a little longer."

The woman was pressed up warm against his back. Rain poured outside the whitewashed cathouse. Raider sure as hell didn't feel like climbing into a saddle and riding all the way to Austin. It was going to take some time to get there, especially if the summer storms kept on stirring the dry plain into mud.

"Raider..."

"I can't, Molly."

"Honey..."

"Don't start. I'm in a bad enough mood as it is."

But Molly didn't have to say a thing. She rested her chin on his shoulder, breathing in his ear. Her hands roamed over the tense sinews of his chest. He let her stay there. He wanted her to talk him out of going. Even if it made him late for his next assignment from Allan Pinkerton.

"Just climb back in with me," she whispered.

He felt himself weakening, but he heard himself say, "I can't."

"Why not?" she asked with a sweet whine.

He gulped for air. "Molly, if I came back to bed, we'd diddle around until it was time for breakfast. And if I had breakfast, my strength would come back and I'd diddle around until lunch. After that, I'd say it was too late in the day to start for Austin, so I might as well stay for dinner."

She eased off. Raider was starting to feel mean. He knew he would feel even worse after an hour in his slicker, trudging through the mire, water dripping off his Stetson.

He pulled on his boots. "Sorry I snapped at you, Molly. You know I ain't like that. It's just, sometimes you have to start somethin' even if you don't want to."

Molly was on his shoulder again. "Stay with me, Raider. This is my house. I'll retire. Nobody but you, honey. You know I been wantin' it that way for the longest time."

He moved away, standing, reaching for his gunbelt. He buckled it around his hip, tying off the holster. His new Colt would probably be a rust ball by the time he got to Austin.

"Troublesome," he moaned. "Just troublesome."

Molly glared at him. "What'd you say about me?"

Raider smiled. "Not you, sweet boogens. You're about ever'thing a man could want. Pretty. Enterprisin'. And sometimes, when I'm with another woman, I think it's you. Like pretendin'."

Her voice cracked a little. "Aw, that's sweet. Then why don't you stay with me?"

He shook his head. "Like I told you, I have my work, just like you have yours. I work for Mr. Pinkerton. I'm a detective."

She drew up her lips in a pout. "Sometimes I think you love your job better'n you love me."

He sat on the bed and took her by the shoulders, pulling her close to him. "Don't ever think I love anybody better'n you, Molly. You're my best girl. One day, when I'm tired of usin' my gun, I'll come back here and we'll both call it quits."

She raised an eyebrow. "What if I find somebody else before then?"

Raider winked. "Then I'll just shoot him."

"I'll bet you would!"

He made her laugh, and they embraced again. Molly kissed him, desperately trying to get him to join her on the warm feather mattress. Raider felt her swaying him, so he had to break away again.

She sighed and leaned back on the pillows. "You're always leavin' me."

"Don't I always come back?"

She went on chattering as Raider looked for his rifle scabbard. Then he remembered that it had been lost while he was chasing the prisoner that had escaped from the New Mexico Territorial Prison. Was it in the canyon? Or the river? His head was muddled.

"Raider, are you listening to me?"

He nodded, reaching for his hat. She started crying when she saw him pick up his Stetson. When he grabbed his hat, it meant that he was really going. She couldn't talk him into staying another day.

"I love you, Molly. I just hope you know that. I ain't said that to more'n a few women in my life. And with you, I mean it."

He turned for the door.

Molly came off the bed, throwing her arms around him. "I love you, too, Raider. Oooh, don't get your fool self killed."

He almost wheeled around and threw her on the mattress. But he couldn't. He had run out of time. He had to go out into the troublesome rain and ride to troublesome Austin to get his next task from the man in Chicago, who could be a damned sight troublesome himself. Pinkerton always threw him into the fire.

He left the flowery scent of Molly's room, tromping down the stairs through the house into the rain. His slicker was in the stable, so he was drenched by the time he got to his mount. The hole in his saddle cinch broke through, and he had to take the time to cut a new one. He also cut his finger.

Raider put the finger in his mouth. The bad feeling was starting up inside him. When the lightning flashed and the thunder sounded overhead, he read the omens in the sky—the ride to Austin was going to be hellacious. He hoped he was wrong, but the thunder and lightning told him different.

Much to his surprise, the rains let up that afternoon. A warm wind blew everything dry. Too dry. The next morning when he woke up, Raider was greeted by pitted gusts of plains wind. He had to tie a bandanna around his face to keep the dirt out his nose. A quick change from bad to worse.

Then the wind shifted back and came from behind him. It seemed to be pushing him along. To what? he wondered.

He finally decided to stop thinking about it and just ride.

"Troublesome," he muttered under his bandanna. "Plain troublesome."

CHAPTER ONE

Dry gusts of hot plains air whipped up whirlwinds on the narrow dirt street of the New Mexico border town. On the weathered porch of a deserted general store, rocking in a wooden rocker, sat a sixty-year-old man in a black suit. He had a bushy gray untrimmed mustache on his face and a black stovepipe hat on his balding pate. Across his lap rested a Remington hammerlock, a twin-barreled scattergun that was primed with buckshot. Leaning against the planked wall of the porch was a shiny .30-caliber Winchester, also loaded to full capacity.

The old gentleman wanted to be ready for anyone who rode out of the flying dust.

Flat Rock, New Mexico, had been a thorn in the side of the territory almost as long as Judge John Farnsworth had been in office. Flat Rock was too far out of the way for any of the lawmen in Albuquerque or Santa Fe. So the governor had left Flat Rock to the judge and the territorial marshal—the late territorial marshal. The few citizens of Flat Rock had fled when they saw the marshal's dead body strung over the back of a horse.

Farnsworth lifted his eyes toward the sounds of some violent commotion. He leveled the scattergun on a whirl of sandy wind. A shutter banged on the cantina. He pulled a plug of tobacco from his coat pocket and bit off a thick chew. He wrapped the tobacco in oil paper and put it in his pocket for later—if later ever came, he thought.

There was trouble in Flat Rock, and now that the marshal was gone the old man had to face it head-on, by himself—unless Providence sent him a miracle.

The judge spat on the porch and started rocking again. He wondered what it was like to be hit by a bullet. Some said it burned. Others said they didn't feel a thing.

He coughed, almost choking on the wad of Virginia plug. Judge John Farnsworth wasn't partial to the idea of dying, but as the last representative of the territorial jurisprudence, he had to stand his ground. The Roundtrees weren't going to make him turn tail and run. Lawlessness along the border had to end, especially if New Mexico was to have a chance at entering the Union.

The judge thumbed back both hammers of the scattergun.

A rider boiled out of the dust, fifty yards in front of the general store. He came slowly toward the judge, plodding on a tall gray. Farnsworth had expected the end to come faster, a sweeping run by at least three of the vermin that Roundtree called hired men.

The stranger kept coming, slow but steady.

Judge Farnsworth stood up. He spat nervously, thinking the gray was out of range for the shotgun. Easing back, he leaned the scattergun against the wall and then picked up the Winchester, thumbing back the hammer behind a full chamber. He expected the rider to break quickly, to go for a moving shot. The judge took aim on the dusty saddle tramp.

"Far enough!" he shouted over the noise of the wind.

A bandanna-covered face peered out from under a wide-brimmed hat. The rider reined back on the gray. The judge watched his hands, anticipating a reply with hot iron. But the man in the saddle simply raised his hands and urged the gray forward with his legs. Farnsworth kept the Winchester on him as the gray came even with the hitching post. A dust-coated hand pulled down the bandanna. His eyes were shiny and cold and black as the night.

The rider broke out with a toothy, loco smile. "Maybe you oughta just shoot me, pardner. Dyin' can't be no worse'n that ride from Santa Fe. This wind has been sandin' me all the way."

Farnsworth was unsure of the man's friendly tone. He motioned with the barrel of the Winchester. "Git on down out of that saddle. But keep them palms up where I can see 'em."

With his hands above his head, the rider kicked his right leg over the saddle horn, bounding to the ground in a single, agile motion. He was so fast that the judge moved back a little. He eyed the stranger, trying to size him up.

The rider looked like any other cowboy. His Stetson was the wide-brimmed kind of a southwestern drifter. Leather vest, thick cotton shirt, faded denim pants, Middleton boots. His face was rugged, but not really evil, except for the coal-tar eyes. He had obviously been on the trail for several days.

Farnsworth's eyes fell on the stranger's sidearm, an oiled Peacemaker low on the hip. The holster had been cut away for fast draw. He probably knew how to use the .45-caliber weapon.

The judge aimed the Winchester in the middle of the man's chest. "Roundtree send you?" He spat after he said it.

The stranger shrugged, starting up the porch steps, keeping his hands toward heaven. "Don't know nobody by that name." He sat down in the rocking chair, seemingly undaunted by the judge's threat to his well-being. "Old man, I'm gonna put my hands down now."

"Can't trust you," Farnsworth replied. "Not as low as you're wearin' that gun."

The stranger only laughed, easing his hands onto the rests of the rocking chair. "Man don't keep his hand near his gun, he don't have long to live in these parts."

Farnsworth considered pulling the trigger.

But the stranger flashed that coyote smile again and said, "S'pose you aim that three-ought someplace else and tell me what I rode into."

The judge shook his head. "Trouble, mister. Just trouble." He studied the stranger closely. "You sure Roundtree didn't send you in here to talk me into leaving?"

"Told you, I don't know no Roundtree." His watchful black eyes spied the jug of corn squeezings that sat on the porch next to the rocker. "I sure am dry, sir. Would you mind if I . . ."

Farnsworth nodded. "Go ahead, dad-blame you." He turned sideways and spat in the street.

"Don't be so agitated, old feller." The stranger lifted the jug to his lips, taking a long swig. He coughed a little as he wiped his mouth with the back of his hand. "Had smoother in my time."

The judge tore the jug from the stranger's hand and drank himself. "It ain't much, but it's free. Thank the good people of Flat Rock. Wherever they are."

The stranger tipped back his Stetson and looked around. "So that's where I am. Flat Rock. Don't like the sound of it. And you're here, havin' trouble with somebody named Roundtree."

"Yep."

"You the law?"

"John Farnsworth, territorial circuit rider. I'm all the law up this way, since the marshal was killed."

The stranger nodded, rocking in the chair. "So what's this Roundtree do that makes you have to face him down?"

"Runs cattle hereabouts."

"Ain't no law agin that," the stranger offered.

"Ain't his cows," the judge replied.

"Rustlin'."

"To name one, cowboy."

The stranger exhaled. "Well, I reckon I better be movin' on, then. Ain't ready for no trouble today."

He started to get up, but Farnsworth kept him in the rocker with the threat of the Winchester. "Can't let you leave."

The stranger's hands were dead still.

"Don't try that iron," the judge said. "You might be quick, but you'd die too if I unload this rifle in your face."

The onyx-black eyes narrowed. "Somethin' on your mind, old man?"

Farnsworth spat tobacco juice. "If you ain't from Round-tree . . ."

"I ain't."

"Then maybe you can help me. I need a gunhand, before it's too late."

"It's too late already, lawman."

The stranger was out of the rocker, rolling forward down the porch steps.

Farnsworth swung the barrel of the Winchester, expecting to meet the bore of the Colt. A slug whizzed by the judge's head, smashing into the wall behind him. But the burst had not come from the stranger. Four riders were barreling out of the dust, the hard-ride attack the judge had figured before. They were swinging Winchesters and howling like Apache warriors.

Farnsworth took aim with the Winchester, hoping to get at least one of them. Another slug knocked off his stovepipe hat before he squeezed the first round. He hit the porch belly down.

The stranger, who had grabbed the reins of the gray, peered back at the judge, shouting, "The rifle, old man!"

Farnsworth tossed him the Winchester, expecting that it would be his last act as a living man.

But the stranger had different notions altogether. He stood behind the gray, steadying the Winchester on the saddle. Farnsworth could not believe his eyes as the rifle barked twice, sending two of the riders straight to hell. Two more bursts from the Winchester sent the third man down. The fourth horseman tried to veer off, but the rifle caused his mount to tumble beneath him.

Farnsworth and the stranger watched as the fourth man staggered to his feet. He reeled for a moment before he straightened himself in the dusty street. His rifle was gone and his hand hung by the butt of an old Navy Colt.

The stranger eased back on the Winchester.

"What are you doin'?" Farnsworth cried. "Plug him!"

The stranger moved away from the shield of the gray. "He wants to call me out, old man. He wants to die right-like."

The two gunmen hesitated in the lull of the wind. As another gust swelled in the street, the last rider went for his pistol. The stranger's Colt streamed fire before the Navy was half out of the holster.

The wounded man stumbled forward, holding the hole on the left side of his chest: dead square in the heart. Dark blood rushed between his fingers. He opened his mouth, which poured crimson instead of words. He tried to raise the Navy, but he could not maintain his balance. He slammed face-first into Flat Rock's only street.

The judge was stunned. He stepped slowly off the porch,

moving even with the stranger. Suddenly Farnsworth laughed
and kicked his feet together in a jig-dance. His hand clapped
the stranger's brawny shoulder.

"Fanciest shootin' I ever seen."

The stranger shrugged away, moving toward his horse. "It
had to be done." He holstered his Colt and grabbed the reins
of the gray.

"Damnedest horse, too," the judge said. "Didn't even
flinch when all the shootin' started."

The stranger swung into the saddle. "Yeah, he's somethin'."

Farnsworth squinted at him. "Where you headin'?"

"Away from here," the stranger replied, turning the gray
east.

"But . . . you can't leave. Not like this!"

Hard, ebony eyes glared down from the back of the gray.
"Roundtree ain't gonna like me killin' those four. Hell, I ain't
even met him yet and I done put some of his men in the
ground. Besides, I got me some business, a lot like your
own."

The judge had to try to stop him. "Look here, Roundtree'll
think I did it. You ain't got to leave yet."

The stranger started forward on the gray. "Ain't much
means more to me than my duty, old-timer. Better that I go."

He was leaving at the same slow pace that had brought him
into town.

The judge ran alongside the gray. "You're fast with that
gun . . ."

"That I am."

"I can pay you, cowboy."

The stranger shrugged, half smiling. "Money don't mean
much to me."

"I need a marshal," Farnsworth hollered.

"I'm already workin' for a big man in Chicago. Name of
Pinkerton."

The grey-haired man was starting to have trouble keeping
up. "I got vittles . . . beef stew!"

"Ain't hungry."

"Dad-blame it, why ain't there a woman around!"

"Sorry, Mr. Lawman."

The judge gasped for breath. "I got good whiskey!"

The gray reined up. The stranger hesitated in the saddle before turning back to the old man. "Better'n that corn liquor?"

"Irish whiskey. I know where the general store man hides it."

The stranger laughed. "Now, you should have said that to me in the first place."

He kicked one leg over the saddle, jumping down. The judge was grinning. As the stranger passed by him, heading for the general store, he handed the reins of the gray to Judge Farnsworth.

"What's your name?" Farnsworth asked.

"Raider," the stranger replied.

The judge followed him, thinking that for now, it was enough that he had coaxed the tall gunslinger into staying.

CHAPTER TWO

John Farnsworth stood by the front window of the general store, peering out at the empty street. The wind had stopped, leaving Flat Rock quiet. Dusk was almost peaceful as it settled down.

The judge spat into an empty tomato can that he held in his right hand. "Looks like they got it all," he called to Raider who was eating at the table across the room. "Liveryman got the live mounts, cantina man got to pick the bodies and keep the dead horse." He laughed a little. "They'll be eatin' horse hereabouts for nigh onto a month."

The tall man hesitated with the spoon he was lifting to his lips. Farnsworth shook his head, vouching for the authenticity of the beef in the stew. Raider put the spoon into his mouth, eating the last bite of tender meat.

"Ain't you never et horse before?" Farnsworth asked.

Raider nodded, swirling a biscuit in the gravy at the bottom of the bowl. "I et horse. I just swore I'd never eat it again after I left Arkansas."

Farnsworth turned away from the window. He struck a sulphur match and put flame to a coal oil lamp that burned orange in the shadows of the general store. He picked up the lamp and joined Raider at the small table.

"Somebody sure as hell taught you how to ride and shoot," the judge said. "They teach you how to read a map?"

Raider leaned forward, nodding, thinking about Pinkerton, who wanted him in Austin.

Farnsworth reached into his coat and took a parchment out of the inside pocket. He unrolled the map and spread it in front of Raider. It was a map of the immediate area. The markings became clearer as Farnsworth pointed them out.

"Borderland," the judge said. "New Mexico on the left, Texas on the right. Roundtree is here, in my jurisdiction."

His weathered finger pointed to a rectangle of land north of Flat Rock. Roundtree's ranch was defined by bold black lines. Dotted lines connected the land to the New Mexico border. The judge told Raider that the borderland had been public property until Roundtree had pushed his claim to the edge of the territorial boundary. No one could stop him. And he had done it primarily to challenge . . .

"Escobar," Farnsworth said. "Here, in Texas." He pointed to the right of the New Mexico border, to a parcel of land that ran up to the border on the Texas side. "Spaniard, Escobar is. Old-timer. Got his original grant from Mexico and then him and his brothers fought with Sam Houston against Santa Anna. Escobar's boy, Miguel, runs the spread now. His father's been in the sickbed for almost ten years. They can't make him die. Tough old cuss."

Raider eyed the judge. "Tough cuss, like you?"

Farnsworth nodded. "Like me."

"How'd Roundtree get his land?" Raider asked.

After he spat in the tomato can, the judge replied, "Bought some of it from homesteaders. Bought it cheap. Shot out the ones who didn't want to sell. He got it all. Then when he pushed his boundaries east to the border, he cut off Escobar's cattle from watering durin' dry spells." He ran his fingertip across a squiggly line on the southern section of the land designated as "Roundtree's." "Spring-fed crick at Three Wells, here. The water ain't far over the border, but Roundtree is dead set on keepin' Escobar out."

Leaning back, the big Pinkerton took his time pouring the corn liquor. After he was quenched, he said, "Been awful dry lately. Makes sense that Escobar's herd would follow their noses to Three Wells. If that happened, then Roundtree might just keep Escobar's cattle."

"Right and wrong," the judge replied. "Right, Escobar's herd did cross over the border. But wrong, Roundtree didn't necessarily keep 'em."

Raider shrugged. "So Escobar ain't lost any cattle?"

"The whole herd disappeared without a trace," Farnsworth replied.

The tall man's brow wrinkled and his eyes squinted ovals of black. "Come again, Judge?"

"Gone, the entire herd. Escobar swears that Roundtree took them while they were watering on his land."

Raider offered the most logical explanation. "Go to Roundtree's spread and look at the herd. Check the brands. If Escobar's brand is there . . ."

"It ain't." The judge decorated the bottom of the tomato can. "Me and . . . the other marshal, we went over ever' inch of Roundtree's ranch. Ain't one of Escobar's cows among them."

"No chance of changin' the brand?" Raider asked.

The judge shook his head and sprinkled a tableau of sugar on the table in front of Raider. He drew Roundtree's brand in the sugar—two parallel lines with a circle at the top. "Round," he said, "and these two lines . . ."

"A tree trunk," Raider replied. "I can see. And Escobar?"

Farnsworth drew a capital "E" with an "S" connecting at the bottom. "No way to make that into the Roundtree brand."

"Nope," Raider agreed. He looked at the map again. "That creek is pretty far south. Anything else around here that I should know about?"

Farnsworth gestured over the map. "Two ranches and three wells. Preacher man lives near the wells with his daughter."

"Anything on Escobar's side?" Raider asked.

The judge shook his head. "No, nothin' really. Some railroad tracks way south, almost two hundred miles. Here. Don't go nowhere, except to hook up with the main line into Austin. Reckon they was crazy when they laid that track."

Raider shrugged. "Maybe. Maybe not." He glared at the judge. "Them cattle are long gone. You really think we can get 'em back?"

Farnsworth turned away, doddering back toward the window on tired legs. He paused at the casement, peering up at the clear black sky. A big moon was sailing into the heavens.

"Blowin' dust is over for a while," the judge said. "But Roundtree ain't gonna stop the storm he's started. Escobar wants to tangle just as bad. Range war ain't a good thing, Raider. Ain't good at all."

The tall man stood up. "Most war ain't. But sometimes it's needed. You sure it's brewin'?"

Farnsworth nodded sadly. "Roundtree's got a thirty-man crew on. Half is cowpunchers, the other half gunslingers. Escobar has a whole bunch of his kin and some old friends of his daddy. Escobar would like to even things for losin' his herd, and Roundtree looks like he wants to fight out of pure damned meanness."

Raider strode to the counter and poured himself a cup of corn liquor. He was thinking as he drank. There was a prisoner in Austin who had to be taken back to Kansas City for a trial. Raider thought he should just go, leave the lawman to handle his own fracas.

He laughed a little. "Judge, I don't know if I ought to be puttin' my ass out on the limb here. Hell, why don't you just go after the militia?"

Farnsworth clapped his hands together in a show of frustration. "I've been to every Army post on both sides of the border. Even the territorial governor wouldn't raise a finger to help me. I'm out here on a limb myself, and the bear is climbin' up the tree to get me."

Raider exhaled, shaking his head. "And you ain't the kind to give up, are you?" He sat down again. "Hell, Judge, I don't think Mr. Pinkerton would cotton to me gettin' mixed up in this. Maybe you oughta just let these two boys, Roundtree and Escobar, shoot it out, settle it amongst theirselves, like the liveryman and the cantina owner."

"Roundtree's doin' wrong!" the judge cried, gagging as he swallowed the plug of tobacco. He hobbled to the counter, coughing, and took a gulp of corn whiskey straight from the jug. "I hate it when I do that. Stuff burns goin' down, and it keeps right on burnin' when it gets there."

Raider tried to hold back his grin. "You're a doublebarreled wonder, Judge."

He glared at Raider. "Ain't nothin' funny about this. But

hell, if you ain't got the liver for it, you can just clear out."

Raider ignored the old man's tone. He was considering the problem. He hated to see a good man like the judge standing up to those that chose to walk on the wrong side of the lawman's fence. Still, the situation sounded hopeless, even for the big man from Arkansas.

Farnsworth bristled, as if he was reading the tall man's mind. "A man like you could make a difference. You're fast with a gun, and you ain't nearly as addlepated as you look. Least you could do is poke your snout around and see what you can root up. And if the bad shootin' starts . . ."

"Didn't know there was such a thing as good shootin'," Raider said.

They were silent for a while.

Raider leaned back, nursing the jug, wondering what to do. Of course, being late wouldn't be a problem. He was late all of the time, and even though he had to listen to Pinkerton's bellyaching, he could always claim the rain had slowed him. It rained a lot in the summer.

Then there would be the problem of the dead bodies if he got into it with his Colt. Bodies always had to be explained to the law. Of course, Judge Farnsworth was the only law on the borderland, so he wouldn't care if a few bullet-riddled outlaws went belly-up.

Then there was the home office to consider. If Wagner or Pinkerton found out that Raider had branched out on his own, his ass could be on train duty or bank duty for a year. But how would they find out? If he stayed around for a few days, how would they know he had helped the old man in the black suit?

Raider shook his head and sighed.

"Get gone, if you can't hack it," the judge said.

"I can hack it."

The old man's eyes sparkled. "You mean . . ."

"I got two days, old man. If we can tie it all up neat-like in that time, we'll do it. Otherwise, I ride on."

"Yes, natural-like. Now the money . . ."

"No money," Raider replied.

"Then why are you . . ."

Raider shrugged. "Let's just say I get a wild hair about people doin' other people wrong."

"Anythin' I can do, Mr. Raider . . ."

"Livery for my mount," the big man replied.

"Yes, sir."

"I want him rubbed down and fed. And I want a bed for myself."

The judge nodded. When he noticed the severity in the tone of Raider's voice, he drew back a little. The congenial cowboy was gone; the stranger had come back, the man who had ridden into Flat Rock on the gray, the fast draw under the Stetson who had cut down four of Roundtree's men.

"What are you plannin'?" the judge asked.

"To sleep," Raider replied.

"Then?"

"Then I go see this Roundtree."

Farnsworth felt an icy stream running along the knots of his spine. Looking at Raider, the old man suddenly found that he felt sorry for Mr. Abel Roundtree. Then he figured Roundtree had brought it all on himself. The judge had a good feeling about the big Pinkerton. Raider might just settle everything. And Farnsworth had a suspicion that the tall man was going to do it with his Colt.

CHAPTER THREE

Light rain fell on Flat Rock the next morning. It was a fine drizzle, enough to wet things down without the huge mud-holes that formed in a downpour. Raider, fresh from a night's sleep, a morning bath, and a change of clothes, stood by the window adjusting his hand-dusted Stetson. His vest and boots were soaped and polished, just like his holster. The Colt on his side was well-oiled, sporting six brass center-fire cartridges in the spotless cylinders. He always filled the sixth chamber for big trouble.

"I feel like a new man, Judge."

"It shows, Raider, it shows. You look almost respectable."

Farnsworth spat into his tomato can.

Behind the counter, the storekeeper muttered beneath his breath. He had come back shortly after midnight and had been complaining to the judge about the way Raider was cleaning him out. The tall man had emptied the pantry after one breakfast. The judge promised payment, and when that didn't shut him up, he reminded the storekeeper that Roundtree might send men to take over the general store if Raider didn't stop him.

Raider fixed a dark blue bandanna around his neck, staring

out the window. Without flinching, he said, "Judge, you ready for company to call this morning?"

Farnsworth hobbled beside him. "Why?"

"Rider comin'," Raider replied. "Just one, though."

The judge picked up his hammerlock shotgun. "Stay back and cover me, Raider. I'll talk to him.'"

Raider stirred a little. "I thought that was my job now."

"Ain't wantin' Roundtree to know about you just yet. Back me up from in here." He hoisted the shotgun and went out onto the front porch.

Raider drew his Colt, wondering if he was going to have a dirty barrel so soon after cleaning it. He watched as the rider came slowly down the lone street. The judge stopped him with one gesture from the Remington.

"Far enough, boy!" the old man cried.

In the saddle of a bay mare sat a kid, a skinny youth with crooked teeth and red spots all over his face. He gawked at the twin barrels of the shotgun. He wouldn't be much trouble, Raider thought. He was just a messenger, a scout.

"Mr. Roundtree sent me," the kid said nervously. "I come to look for Hank and the others."

Farnsworth spat tobacco in the street. "Hank and t'others are dead, boy."

The kid's voice came out weakly. "Dead?"

"Yep," Farnsworth said. "I kilt 'em. And you can go back and tell your bossman that I'll shoot anybody else he sends after me." He unleashed a brown stringer to punctuate his declaration.

The kid broke into an uncertain smile. "Aw, you're just pullin' my leg, Granpa. I bet Hank put you up to this."

The judge yelled, "Git gone!" and then unloaded both barrels of the scattergun into the air. The bay mare reared and bolted away from the blast, taking the gangly kid back to Roundtree's ranch. Raider holstered his Peacemaker and stepped out next to the judge, wishing his ex-partner was still around. He could have used Doc's sage advice and guidance —even though he was sure the retired Mr. Weatherbee would not approve of his acting alone.

Farnsworth was smiling. "That oughta put a burr under Roundtree's ever-lovin' saddle."

Without a word, Raider stepped off the porch and started across the street for the livery.

"Where you goin'?" Farnsworth called.

"To make sure the cantina man ain't servin' my horse for breakfast."

Farnsworth came down a few steps off the porch. "Raider!"

As the big man turned, he could see the glistening silver of the coin that Farnsworth had tossed toward him. Raider caught the silver dollar and looked at it in his hand.

He scowled at the old man. "I told you, I ain't wantin' no money."

"For luck," Farnsworth called.

Raider nodded and put the silver dollar in his vest. Luck was something he knew about. Something he needed plenty of.

"I'm on my way, Judge. Thanks a heap."

"Just keep it on you," Farnsworth replied. "You never know when it might come in handy."

Raider remembered that Doc had never believed in luck. He waved to the old man before he turned and went on to the livery. Doc hadn't always been right about everything. Especially when it came to the winding wheel of Lady Fortune.

The gray pounded the moist turf, racing over the rolling acres of thick grassland. Raider was heading north, toward Three Wells. He had the judge's map in his saddlebag, but before he thought he might have to use it, he ascended a rise and looked down into a natural basin.

In the hollow of the basin rested a small twig-and-plaster structure. The preacher man's church, judging by the cross on the roof. Raider could see two horses tied up at a hitching post in front of the church. There were no other signs of life.

Raider urged the gray down the slope, reining back as the animal slowly found its way. When he was on flatland again, he spurred the gray into a gallop, driving for the church. He was a hundred yards away when he saw them.

Two cowboys were dragging a struggling man out of the plaster dwelling. The struggling man's hands were tied behind him. Raider reined up about twenty yards away from them. When the cowboys caught sight of him, they let go of their captive, who fell to the ground, moaning. Both men had side-arms, and they positioned themselves as if they knew how to use them.

Raider's hand hung loosely by his hip as he called, "What's goin' on here?"

A snaggled-toothed man in a brown duster held up a rope. "We're hangin' this preacher."

Raider eased the gray into a walk, coming toward them, never taking his eyes off their hands. He reined up about ten yards away. Both gunmen were still, anticipating a challenge from Raider, who jumped out of the saddle and squared his shoulders.

The second hangman, a skinny, ferret-faced man with a pointed hat, turned full front to Raider. He was confident of his gunhand. It showed in his face and his stance. His voice came out as a challenge. "You got somethin' agin us hangin' this no-account preacher?"

Raider shrugged, watching them for any signs of quick movement. "If he's done somethin' wrong, we'll take him in front of the judge."

Both of them laughed.

The snaggle-toothed man raised the rope again. "Only judge we need is right here."

The pointed hat added, "'Tain't no judge around here noways. He's done been killed."

Raider's eyes narrowed. "You Roundtree's men?"

The hangmen looked at each other. Then the man in the pointed hat grinned. "We work for Mr. Roundtree. You wouldn't be Johnny Dallas, would you? New hand up from Phoenix?"

Raider informed them that he was not Johnny Dallas.

The two men looked at each other again. Raider could feel it building, the tension in their hands. He told them he was the new lawman and that they should back away from the fallen man.

The pointed hat man replied, "Make us."

The next sound was the rustling of the rope as it dropped from the hands of the snaggle-toothed man. Sleeves rustled as the pointed-hat man went for hot iron. Raider moved quicker. Two bursts from his Colt bloodied their chests.

The skinny man in the pointed hat stumbled backward,

trying to lift an old Remington pistol. Raider shot the pistol out of his hand. The pointed hat rolled away when the man fell on his back. He gulped air for a few seconds and then died.

The snaggle-toothed man passed on a little more quietly.

The Colt was still smoking as Raider dropped it back into his holster. He stepped over the body of the snaggle-toothed man to help the live man on the ground. Raider pulled a bandanna gag off the man's mouth.

"Thank you, sir," the man said in a weak tone. "Praise the Lord. Thanks be to Jesus for sendin' you, my deliverer."

"Jesus didn't send me," Raider replied. "Judge Farnsworth did."

The man had a frail face, eggshell white skin, and gray sprinkled in his thin head of hair. Pointed chin, deep-set eyes, brow lined from a perpetual state of worry.

"You the preacher?" Raider asked.

"Yes, praise God. If you would be so kind as to untie me, sir."

Raider shook his head. "Not until you tell me why them two was fixin' to lynch you."

"Yes, certainly," the preacher replied. "I'm glad you asked. It wouldn't have been right not to show some caution, after all. . . ."

Raider heard thrashing and muffled screams from inside the church. He went to the doorway of the hovel and pulled back a moth-eaten cloth. A young woman was hog-tied in front of the altar, lying on the dirt floor. She wore a Mexican blouse and a plain, dark skirt. Raider felt warm all of a sudden.

"She's my daughter," the preacher called. "Please don't hurt her. Don't take advantage of . . ."

Stepping into the small hovel, Raider lifted the woman in his arms. He carried her outside and dropped her next to her father. The preacher begged for Raider to untie both of them.

"Not till you tell me what this hangin' was about," he replied.

The preacher gladly delineated the same story told by the judge—the conflict over boundaries and watering rights, and the vanished herd. The preacher sided with Escobar, as his late wife had been one of Escobar's distant cousins. The preacher's alliance with Escobar and his influence with some of the local people had been enough for Roundtree to order his execution.

"After all," the preacher offered, "it is God's water. Shouldn't everyone be able to use it?"

"Sounds like Roundtree ain't gonna be happy till he's put everybody out of his way."

Raider looked at the girl. She was glaring up at him with hateful brown eyes that might have been more appealing if they were softer. Her dark skin and jet black hair came from her mother's side. The big Pinkerton tried to keep himself from thinking how pretty she was. She couldn't have been a day past seventeen.

"All right," he said finally. "I'll untie you."

The girl tried to attack him when she was free. Raider fended off her fists until her father was able to subdue her. She spat at Raider, calling him one of Roundtree's dogs. The preacher apologized for his daughter and introduced himself as Elias Newton. His daughter's name was Maria.

Raider told them his name and said that he was trying to help the judge solve the riddle of the missing herd.

"I know the judge," Newton said. "He is a good man. And you must be a good man too, Mr. Raider. Thank God. Thank God for good men. Why, the way you took care of those two scalawags. Maria, go make us some coffee."

The girl reluctantly obeyed, still not ready to believe in the tall Pinkerton.

Over steaming clay mugs, Preacher Newton explained how he had come to take over the old Spanish mission at Three Wells. He had built a small but devoted congregation among the homesteaders and some of the local Indians. But when Roundtree had moved into the valley, the homesteaders had left, and the Indians stopped attending his services after Roundtree's men had shot up the place one Sunday. When Newton still refused to leave, two of Roundtree's men had come to hang him.

Raider leaned back. "More I hear about this Roundtree, the more I don't like him. Seems he's wantin' to pick on the weak-like. No offense, Preacher."

The preacher raised his hand. "Blessed are the meek, for they shall inherit the earth." Newton's eyes were bulging expectantly. "So you're the new marshal. Last one didn't make it for long."

Raider ignored the remark. "You say you married one of Escobar's kin a while back?"

Newton nodded. "A second cousin. She passed on from cholera about five years after Maria was born. A good woman. Loved the Lord better'n most."

"Take me to Escobar," Raider said flatly.

Newton's thin face flushed red. "I couldn't. Oh no. I can't even ride. And you must know that Escobar never accepted me. Besides, it would take the rest of the day for us to get there, even if I could ride. I don't think—"

"I will take him."

Maria stood next to the table, staring at the big man from Arkansas.

"Didn't think you liked me," Raider offered.

"I was wrong," she replied. "I can see now that you are a good man. I will take you there."

"No!" her father cried. "I cannot allow it."

"The way you could not allow those men to hang us," Maria replied. "I will take Mr. Raider to my cousin. Miguel knows me. He will listen."

Newton bristled like a banty rooster. "Your cousin wants you to stay in his house like a servant. I will not allow this."

She began to curse in Spanish.

Raider shook his head. "Your pa's right, Maria. You can't go there. It'd be too dangerous. But you can show me the way, point me in the right direction. When I get there, I'll tell your cousin Miguel that you sent me."

She nodded, still fuming, avoiding his gaze with her brown eyes.

Raider wondered if he should trust her. He could never tell what a woman was thinking. It was one of his few weaknesses, but he knew from experience that it could be a fatal one.

Allan Pinkerton sat down at his desk. A fresh cup of coffee steamed next to the sheaf of papers that had been brought from the chief clerk of records in the Pinkerton National Detective Agency. Pinkerton always needed a cup of coffee to brace him through an arduous task like reading Raider's file.

The rough-hewn agent had also submitted another report, a terse chicken-scratch exercise in linguistic simplicity.

Pinkerton unfolded the latest dispatch from the big man from Arkansas. Written in lead pencil, the report said only: "I caut Billy Ray Greevus and kilt him fore he tried to kill me." Below that was the seal of the territorial marshal, Cheyenne, Wyoming. The marshal had written: "Mr. Raider had no help from us and did this all by his own self. We are grateful to him."

"Barbaric," Pinkerton admitted to himself. "But he did the job."

He leafed through Raider's file. Known name: *Raider*. Home state: *Arkansas*. Age: *Unknown, between thirty and forty*. Number of men killed: *Unknown, estimated between fifty and four hundred*.

There wasn't a better shootist among his agents. Raider was quick. He had the gift of anticipation. With his former partner, he had been unstoppable. Now that he was working alone, he did not seem to be slowing down at all. A useful man.

Pinkerton looked up when the door to his office swung open. "Wagner."

Wagner, Pinkerton's right-hand man, stepped into the dim office. "It's getting dark outside," he said, striking a match for the gas lamps on the wall behind Pinkerton's desk.

When the lamps were glowing, Wagner looked back at the file in front of Pinkerton. "Raider, huh."

"Don't sound so disgusted," Pinkerton rejoined. "He saved your life once, remember?"

Wagner nodded. He wanted to forget about the incident with the prize-fighter, when he had been duped by an unscrupulous policeman in Kansas City. Ironic that they now needed Raider in Kansas City, as soon as they got word to him in Austin. He was bringing up the prisoner anyway.

Wagner sat down in an easy chair. "Are you sure Raider's the one for this job? He can be a bit brutal. Bodies strewn about and all that."

Pinkerton sighed. "We'll see the end of his kind one day."

"I'm sure," Wagner replied. "Men will stop carrying guns. They already have here in Chicago."

Pinkerton closed the file. "But men still carry guns, so we

need him now, Wagner. We need him now."

Wagner leaned back, remembering Raider's fast gunhand. "Yes, we sure as hell do need him, I suppose. We will until . . ."

Pinkerton eyed his subordinate. "Say it."

". . . until he's killed."

Pinkerton only nodded, a peculiar look in his tired eyes, like a man who has stared too long at a chessboard.

CHAPTER FOUR

As Raider followed the girl into Texas, he kept his eyes open. He never liked going against superior odds, especially to come between two sides that were warring against each other. He would at least assess the situation before he fired any shots. Maybe he could even straighten things out. Hell, how many times had a case come down to one well-placed bullet or a handily tossed stick of red dynamite? Maybe the judge was right—one man could make a difference.

Raider's black eyes focused on the saddle of the nag that Maria urged along the trail. He tried not to dwell on the tattered cloth skirt that rode the dark skin of her thighs. Her backside bounced off the leather with the slightest jiggle of firm youth. Was she deliberately letting the thin white blouse fall off her brown shoulders? She had also let her hair down, and it swung over the smooth surface of her back.

The big man shook off the surge inside himself. He eased his mount next to her and spoke without looking at her face. "How much longer?"

She shrugged, the slightest hint of a pouty smile lodged on her full mouth. "I cannot be sure. My cousin's ranch is just beyond those hills."

Raider reined up, peering into the distance. He saw the

slow rise of the plain extending into a series of lumpy ridges that wouldn't pass for hills anywhere but in Texas. His hand brushed the butt of his Colt in a reflexive gesture.

"What is wrong?" Maria asked.

Raider exhaled. "Nothin'. Leastways nothin' I can put my finger on. It's just . . . hills like that can be a good place for bushwhackers."

"But you are coming to help my cousin," she offered.

"Yeah, but he don't know that." Raider glanced at her.

Maria smiled. He couldn't understand the grin until his eyes fell below her waist. The ragged skirt had ridden up above her thighs, giving him a full view of the hairy wedge below her stomach. He turned his eyes away after a nervous look.

Maria laughed. "Why not, cowboy? We could do it right here."

"Because you're the preacher's daughter," Raider grumbled. "And you ain't nothin' but a girl nohow."

"I am a woman!"

"Sure." He gestured back from where they came. "You best ride back to your daddy. He'll—"

"Hah! He talks about his God, a God he has never seen. A God that keeps me from my . . ."

Raider bristled, casting a hasty glance to the sky. "Don't be badmouthin' the Lord, little lady."

"Why not?"

"'Cause He's liable to kick your sinnin' ass if He . . ."

With complete disregard for Raider's lecture, Maria spurred the nag forward, driving toward the hills in the distance. Raider grunted and started to spring after her. But he slowed up finally, thinking she would not get far, even though the nag was surprisingly fast. Raider wanted to save his own mount for later if he had to run.

The hills looked a lot bigger when he reached them. He guided his mount into a natural crevice between two slopes. The big man expected to hear Maria's laughter as she taunted him from some hiding place. But he didn't hear a thing.

"Woman!" he shouted.

There was the slightest echo in the hills.

Raider stopped the gray, listening.

Where the hell was she?

"All right, Maria, cut the malarkey."

No reply.

"I mean it."

He was becoming irritated.

"Your last chance, otherwise I tell your daddy."

Maybe she was gone. Maybe she knew some route out of the hills that would take her back around him. Raider urged the gray forward between the mounds of earth. He expected to find her around one of the blind corners, waiting with that skirt pulled up to her . . . If he wasn't in the middle of trouble, he would have . . .

Raider pulled back on the reins. What had he heard? A voice? Or was it scuffling on the trail?

"All right, Maria, I've about had it with this shit."

But it wasn't the girl that he heard.

Suddenly Raider was surrounded by the chortling levers of oiled Winchester rifles. He froze, his hand hovering over the butt of the Colt. His eyes picked out the silhouette against the bright sky—a lanky figure with a sombrero and a rifle barrel aimed straight at him.

"I don't think I would try to use your weapon, señor."

They had him surrounded in the gully. Four of them on the crests of the ridges on all sides. Even with a good-sighted Winchester he wouldn't have been able to get them all. At least they wanted him alive. Otherwise he would have been dead already.

"I'm ready to talk," Raider hollered. "I'm here about Escobar."

The men called back to each other in Spanish before they ordered Raider to drop his gun. He hated letting his Colt hit the ground, but it was a healthy alternative to catching a load of rifle lead. When he was unarmed, a small man stepped from the rocks to pick up the Peacemaker.

Raider peered down at the face under the sombrero. "Can you take me to Escobar?"

Without replying, the man grabbed the reins of the gray and started to lead it forward. Raider wondered if they had the girl. Escobar wouldn't harm his own kin, he thought. Then it crossed his mind that she might have set him up. A trap.

When they came out of the hills, Raider saw them gathered around a campfire. Thirty-odd men shifted their eyes toward him. Someone asked if he was Johnny Dallas. Raider replied that he was not, and then, when pressed with further questions, he told them he was only going to speak to Miguel Escobar himself.

No one paid him any heed until he said that he might have a way for Escobar to get his cows back. Then two men in sombreros talked for a few minutes, arguing in Spanish. Raider wasn't sure what they were saying. He got a little nervous when they decided to tie his hands behind his back. At first he thought they might be going to hang him. But as it turned out, they were only taking precautions before they led him to the veranda of Miguel Escobar's stucco hacienda.

"Are you sure that no message has come in from Texas?" asked Allan Pinkerton. "No word at all from Raider?"

Wagner shook his head. "Nothing."

"Damn." Pinkerton looked out the window for a moment. "Where was the point of origin for the last message?"

"Santa Fe," Wagner replied, adjusting his spectacles.

Pinkerton got up and strode to the map of the territories west of Chicago. "All of those square miles for Raider to get lost in."

Wagner scoffed. "If he is lost."

Pinkerton turned around. "You don't have to remind me of Raider's whoring and drinking."

"Gambling, too," Wagner said. "He's probably holed up in some hacienda with a deck of cards in his hand."

Pinkerton laughed almost fondly.

Wagner eyed him suspiciously. "Usually Raider has you baffled and angry. Don't tell me you're starting to like him."

"Like him?" Pinkerton replied. "No, I don't like him. I envy him."

Wagner's eyes bugged out. "That galoot! He's a saddle tramp. No ambition. If you hadn't given him gainful employment, he'd still be drifting, picking up a job here or there, punching cattle."

Pinkerton gestured toward the window. "He's out *there*, Wagner. He's living while we're inside these walls growing old."

"We have a lot more chance of living to be a ripe old age," Wagner replied. "If you ask me, Doc Weatherbee did the right thing by retiring. Raider would have gotten him killed sooner or later."

"They were quite a team."

Someone knocked on the door.

"Come in," Pinkerton called, expecting a telegram from Austin.

"Your newspaper, sir," said a young lad.

Pinkerton tipped him a penny and threw the paper on the desk.

"Aren't you going to read it?" Wagner asked.

Pinkerton shook his head. "Later. I'm too nervous now. As you know, this case we're handing to Raider involves the brother of one of my best friends from the old days."

"Well, don't worry," Wagner said, scowling, "Raider will probably find a way to endanger the lives of all involved."

Miguel Escobar was thin and wiry, like a coachwhip snake. His eyes were blacker than Raider's and flashed brightly whenever he spoke. He had slicked-back hair, a thin mustache, and was clad all in black, with a mirrored sombrero hanging on his back. He pointed down from his veranda with a coiled bullwhip.

"You! Gringo!" he shouted at Raider. "You are Johnny Dallas. You were sent here by Roundtree to kill me. I have heard your name all over this territory."

Raider frowned. "You know, I'm awful tired of people tellin' me that I'm this Johnny Dallas. My name is Raider. I'm a Pinkerton operative workin' on special assignment for Judge Farnsworth, territorial marshal of New Mexico. Leastways in the land just over your border, he's the only law."

Escobar's eyes were slitted in the bright sun. "Farnsworth?" he said hesitantly. "A judge?"

"A judge that's on your side,' " Raider replied. "Just like me. I come here to talk to you about losin' your herd. Maybe there's a way I can help you get it back."

Escobar spoke in Spanish to one of the five gunmen who flanked him to the right and left. Then he challenged the big man again. "Why would this Farnsworth want to help me?"

Raider shifted on his heels. "Well, it ain't so much he wants to help you as he wants to prevent a range war and get rid of Roundtree."

"How do you know so much of this if you are not working for Roundtree?"

"I rode smack-dab into it," Raider said. "Next thing I know, your cousin Maria is leadin' me right—"

Escobar bristled. "Maria! What have you done to her?"

"I ain't done—"

The bullwhip cracked beside Raider's ear. The big man's eyebrows slanted in. Escobar was beginning to get on his nerves.

"Where is my cousin?" Escobar demanded.

Raider scowled back at him. "I might ask you the same thing, pardner. One minute she's tellin' me she's gonna fix me up so I can talk to you, and the next minute she's—"

"You killed her!" the rancher cried. "There were two people killed at the mission. I have heard the truth."

"Yeah," Raider offered. "Two of them got it. But they was Roundtree's men. I plugged them myself. Your cousin is alive and kickin', and so is her daddy."

"Lies!"

Raider shook his head. "Only thing I can tell you is send some of your boys to check with her pa. If I'm tellin' the truth about that, then I'm straight and square on wantin' to help you."

Escobar glanced back at a gray-haired man who seemed to be the second one in charge. The gray-haired man nodded. Escobar looked back at Raider.

He pointed with the whip. "Very well, gringo. I will send a man to see if you are as you say. But if I find that you are lying, I will cut the life out of you with this whip."

Raider met his forceful gaze with a hateful stare. "And if I ain't lyin', Miguel, maybe you and me can toe the line for a fistfight."

"Take him to the cellar!"

Two caballeros led Raider to a dark cell beneath the stucco house. He was locked in, his hands still tied. It took Raider a couple of minutes to work the knot loose. When his hands were free, he examined the cellar for escape possibilities. There was one small window that a weasel would have trouble getting through.

Raider sat down on the dirt floor, leaning back against the stones of the basement wall. His head was suddenly blank. He did not waste time chiding himself for being so stupid. He would simply have to wait until the right moment—if it ever came.

His eyes fell on a rack at the other side of the cellar. He saw the round ends of wine bottles sticking out between the wooden slats. Raider had never liked wine much, even though some swore that it was better than good whiskey. He took one dusty bottle out of the rack and fiddled with the cork until he managed to push it down into the bottle. He gulped a few mouthfuls and wiped his lips with the back of his hand. It would never replace red-eye, he thought, but at least his head began to buzz a little.

He finished the bottle and lay back on the dirt floor. His eyes burned a little and his throat was dry. He wondered how long it would take for Escobar to find out that he was there to help.

The big man dozed off and on in a cell where most men would have been unable to sleep. He woke up after dark, squinting in the blackness. Even the dim glow from the window had disappeared. Or had it?

Raider saw a flickering by the portal. A small round face flashed at the opening. Footsteps coming down the stairs to the cellar. A hand worked the latch on the other side of the door.

Pressing himself against the wall, Raider waited for the shadowy figure to enter the cellar. He figured he had a chance in the dark. If he could just knock out the guard and take his gun. Unless, of course, there were coming to get him to tell him that everything was all right. The moment of hesitation did not hurt him.

A candle slipped through the doorway, illuminating the basement. Behind the flame came the smooth, chubby face of one Maria Newton, the preacher's daughter and cousin to Miguel Escobar. When her dark eyes turned to Raider, he grabbed her and put his hand over her mouth.

"What the hell are you doin' here?" he whispered.

She bit his palm, forcing him to remove his hand. "I came to help you, you fool. I will speak to my cousin."

"Yeah, well, he thinks I done killed you and your pappy, too."

She smiled. "I will tell him the truth."

Raider eased around her, peering out of the open door. "Maybe I don't feel like waitin' till you clear my good name."

"You'd never get away," Maria replied. "My cousin has men all over the ranch. They'd kill you before you reached the stable."

Raider closed the door and turned back to her. "Then git upstairs and tell your cousin that I ain't one of Roundtree's men."

Her thick coral lips parted in a devious smile. She shifted on her feet, her eyes wide in the candlelight. A line of sweat had broken out on her upper lip. She inched the skirt up toward her stomach.

"Whoa, Maria," he said. "What are you . . ."

She licked the sweat from her upper lip. "You want something from me, I want something from you."

"No!"

She knelt down, putting the candle down carefully on the floor. Those brown eyes turned up at him. "I know you want me. I saw you on the trail. You were hard every time you looked at me. I could see you through your pants."

"That don't mean nothin'."

She stretched out on her back, the skirt around her waist, her dark thighs parted. "Hurry, cowboy. Before my cousin finds us."

"Damn it all."

But she was getting to him. He felt it in his pants, just like she had said. As he unbuttoned his fly, he wondered if he would go to Hell for nailing a preacher's daughter. He pulled his pants down around his thighs and dropped on one knee beside her.

She reached out for his cock. "Hurry," she said breathlessly. "Put it inside me."

He touched the smooth skin of her thigh. "Not so fast. A man has to stroke a woman. Like she's a cat or somethin'. He has to get her ready."

Her hand tugged at the rigid shaft between his legs. "I am ready."

His finger explored the wetness of her crevice. "Yeah, I reckon you are. You are at that."

He positioned himself in the notch of her thighs. Her hands guided him into position. He entered her slowly, allowing her to adjust to the size of his prick. His mouth strayed down to kiss her taught nipples. She groaned and pulled his face back so she could kiss him.

"So big," she moaned.

Her words dwindled into a short lapse of breath. Raider found his rhythm, forgetting everything but his own need. Her buttocks bounced off the hard floor as he rose and fell.

When her face contorted and he felt the tightening deep within her, Raider released himself, driving his discharge into her, forcing a series of quivering climaxes that shook her body. He was afraid someone might hear Maria's moans, so he put his hand over her mouth again. This time she did not bite him.

She brushed his hand away and put her lips close to his ear. "Never have I had a man so big as you."

Raider rolled off. "Yeah, I'm glad you liked it. Now how about goin' to tell your cousin that he shouldn't kill me."

She laughed wickedly. "Not until I'm finished."

"What are you gonna . . ."

She explored, playing with him like he was a toy. Raider tried to resist, but he figured she wouldn't give up until she had her way. So they rolled around on the cellar floor until Raider landed on top again. He penetrated her and accomplished the same pleasurable result of their first coupling.

When he rolled off the second time, he said, "You had enough?"

She kissed him and replied, "As if you did not enjoy it."

Raider grunted. "Yeah, I did. But there's a lot more goin' on here than a hot-tailed young chippy gettin' her oats. If you don't run upstairs and set things straight with your cousin, then my ass is in the icehouse for certain. *Comprende?*"

She pushed her body away from him. "Damn you, Raider. Must men always be so single-minded?"

He put his hand behind her head, pulling her close so he could kiss her. "You get me upstairs to see your cousin and I'll do anything you say, lady. Now get gone."

She stood up and dusted off her skirt, pulling it down over her bushy wedge. "I will go to my cousin. He will do as I say. He always does what I tell him."

Raider's eyebrows slanted in. "How can you be sure of that?"

Her face slacked into a knowing frown. "I will make him do it. The same way I made you please me. Only. . ."

"Somethin' wrong?"

She picked up the candle, hurrying out of the cellar without a reply.

Raider shook his head. He figured he didn't have any right to judge her. People weren't always the way you wanted them to be. And if she got him out of the smelly dungeon, he didn't care what she did to her cousin.

"Good Lord, Wagner, look at this."

Allan Pinkerton held out the newspaper for his associate. Wagner grabbed the periodical, a weekly paper from Texas. As part of their agency's library, Pinkerton had papers and magazines sent to Chicago from all over the country. The paper in question hailed from Austin, Raider's proposed destination.

Wagner read the headline: "'Rumors of Range War Fire Militia Talk; Governor Refuses to Commit Troops.'"

Wagner looked at Pinkerton. "I don't find this significant."

Pinkerton gestured to the huge map on the wall. "Raider's last communication was from Santa Fe, New Mexico. Here."

"So, I don't—"

"If he were coming south," Pinkerton continued, "he would come right through this region. Here."

Wagner studied the story in the newspaper. "Says here that the range war rumors are hailing out of northwestern Texas, near the New Mexico border. Near a place called Flat Rock."

Pinkerton nodded. "Raider's there."

"How can you be sure?" Wagner asked, ripping off his spectacles.

"An instinct," Pinkerton replied. "If there's trouble near there, where else would he be? I wonder if we could wire the local authorities to be on the lookout for him."

Wagner's nose went back into the paper. "Says here that the authorities aren't acknowledging the range war. They claim it doesn't exist."

Pinkerton studied the map again. "If only there were some way to get some help in there. At times like these, I wish that big hillbilly was still partners with Doc Weatherbee."

"But he's not," Wagner replied flatly.

Pinkerton sighed, his eyes still on the map. "No, he's not. I'm afraid he's on his own."

"Maybe he isn't there after all," Wagner offered.

But they both knew better.

The candle appeared at the tiny window about two hours after Maria had left him. She eased through the door, smiling weakly. She was carrying a tray.

"Am I free?" Raider asked.

She nodded and told him that her cousin would let him out first thing in the morning.

"The mornin'!" Raider squawked. "You mean I got to sleep on this dirty floor for a whole night?"

Maria handed him the tray. "Here. I brought you food. Eat. You will need your strength."

Raider devoured the beans and rice and sliced beef. He could not remember when he had tasted anything as good. When he put down his plate, he saw the look in Maria's brown eyes.

She tilted her head a little. "Are you feeling strong?"

He laughed. "One more time, huh?"

She lowered her eyes. "I cannot stay the whole night. My cousin . . . Miguel expects me to come back to his bed."

She reached for the buttons of his pants.

"Ain't you had enough between the both of us?" Raider asked good-naturedly. "I mean, hell . . . hey, don't look like that. I mean, I didn't want to hurt your feelin's, honey."

Her face had slacked into a serious, frightened expression. "It's all right," she said softly. "It's just . . . the things Miguel does to me . . . they don't . . . I'm not . . . satisfied."

Raider touched her shoulder. "We don't have to do nothin' if you don't want to, Maria."

She rubbed his cheek against the back of his hand. "No, it is the way I want it. With you. Now."

He put his arms around her and held her for a long time before they finally stretched out on the floor.

CHAPTER FIVE

Miguel Escobar stared across the breakfast table at the big, black-eyed stranger. Raider had his grizzled face in a plate of eggs and potatoes, his third helping besides the whole loaf of fresh bread that had disappeared. Raider had not been able to resist the recently churned butter.

When he had finished eating, Raider downed two cups of coffee and asked for a third. Escobar had coffee as well, a thick, black, steaming liquid. It gave Raider a jolt.

He scowled at Escobar. "I ain't happy about sleepin' in that basement all night."

Escobar shrugged. "A man cannot be too careful. Allow me to extend the full hospitality of my hacienda."

Raider nodded. "All right, I'll take that like you said you're sorry."

Escobar frowned.

"Don't get upset on me, Mr. Escobar," Raider said. "I just want you to know that I am who I say."

"A Pinkerton agent?" Escobar replied. "Sometimes your reputations precede you. Some would say you're rather un-scrupulous in your pursuit of the hunted."

Raider leaned back in the chair. "You want your cattle back? Or not?"

"I'm listening," replied the dubious host.

Raider asked for maps of the region. He had Escobar mark off his land and then the place where his herd had last been seen. Raider nodded. He asked Escobar to tell him how the herd was taken.

The night riders had been killed, and the herd had been shuffled away in the darkness. The trail led to the water on Roundtree's land and stopped there. There had been no tracks on the other side of the creek. It had been as if Roundtree had made the herd disappear.

Raider fired off a series of questions to which Escobar responded.

"Where did you search for your cows?"

"On Roundtree's land."

"And you didn't find them?"

"No."

"Did he act like he wasn't wantin' you to poke around?"

"He invited us to come onto his spread. Damn it, I know he took those cattle. He must have covered his trail somehow."

Raider shook his head. "You can't cover up the tracks of a whole herd of cows. How many head did you have?"

"Three thousand. I was going to drive them to market."

Raider pointed at the map. "The same thing that old Roundtree's going to do. And I think we can catch him."

Escobar leaned forward, politely laying a bone-handled Colt .45 on the table. "Perhaps you should explain yourself."

Raider ignored the Colt. "Look at the creek here. It runs back to this little river. All Roundtree had to do was take them cows up the water to the river. There he crosses over, no tracks, cows gone."

Escobar's eyes grew wider. "Yes. Yes! Why didn't I see that?"

Raider frowned a little. "Why didn't you see that I'm on your side?"

Escobar stood up and bowed to Raider. It was something a gentleman would do.

Raider shook his head. "Don't be gettin' fancy on me, Miguel."

Apparently the Spanish rancher had no intention of letting anything get past him. "Say you are telling the truth, Señor

Raider. Where are my cattle? What did Roundtree do when he got the herd past the river?"

"Nothin'," Raider replied, throwing out his hands. "Not for a while anyway. He lays low, lets you look the place over. Meanwhile, your herd is sittin' no more'n twenty-five miles northeast of here, on the Texas side. How long ago was your herd taken?"

Escobar counted on his fingers. "Six days ago."

Raider gestured toward the map. "Then I figure he oughta be about here. East of us, headin' south."

Escobar pored over the maps. "South for what?"

"The railroad tracks," Raider replied. "It's a new commotion. Sendin' cows on railroad cars to market. Looks like old Roundtree is gonna give it fair country try."

Escobar stood up and strutted back and forth like a rooster. "Impossible, I tell you."

Raider put his hands behind his head. "Well, yeah, I reckon it does sound farfetched. But that's the only way he coulda done it. And he's sneakin' your cows right behind your back."

Escobar threw out the hand that he had used to hold the whip. "All right, I'm willing to believe you. Tell me how I am to regain my herd. My men and I are behind you."

"May not need your men," Raider repiled. "Though it would be best to bring 'em along in case things don't work out. We might have to shoot it out with Roundtree, but not if I can help it."

Escobar asked, "How can you avoid a fight?"

"I won't be able to if we don't get out of here right now," Raider replied. "Have you got a lot of fast horses?"

"Yes."

"Get 'em hitched. We got to ride south. We got to beat Roundtree to the railroad."

Escobar smiled for the first time. *Madre Dios*, I believe you have roped the calf, Mr. Raider."

"One more thing," the big man said.

"Yes?" Escobar replied.

"Have you got any dynamite?"

They rode southeast, to the railroad tracks on Escobar's map. An army of Escobar's men accompanied the big Pinkerton, although Miguel made sure he rode point as the unquestioned leader. Raider wondered if Miguel would give in if forced to do things Raider's way. The big man hoped that he could avoid a confrontation.

When they reached the tracks, the train was waiting there. Raider identified himself to the engineer and told them that they were going to recover some stolen cows. The engineer and the conductor both disclaimed any knowledge of a rustled herd. They were simply there to take the cows east. Both agreed to cooperate to the letter of the law.

So Raider and the small army sat down to wait.

They waited for the rest of the day and the next morning. Escobar was getting impatient. Raider was nervous himself, having taken a day longer than he had intended.

"They aren't coming!" Miguel railed. "I was loco to listen to you, gringo. You were lying to me."

He rattled the lever of a silver-plated Winchester.

Raider squinted at the bore of the rifle. "Save your bullets, Miguel. Something's coming yonder."

A rider, one of Escobar's men, rode in on a lathered black gelding. He spoke to his boss in Spanish. Escobar nodded and then looked at Raider.

"The herd is coming, gringo." He held up the silver-plated Winchester. "Now Roundtree pays."

Raider pulled the rifle back down. "Easy, Miguel. We have to time this just right. Otherwise the whole thing could blow up in our faces."

"You will not deny me killing Roundtree!" Escobar cried.

"Roundtree will get his," Raider replied. "But until I give the word, we do it my way first."

"No!"

"Otherwise I walk out of here right now and you could lose your herd a second time."

Escobar nodded reluctantly.

The herd came closer.

Roundtree was riding point himself. Escobar pointed him out to Raider. He also identified a kid in a white Stetson. Johnny Dallas. Raider figured to have a talk with that boy.

Escobar's men were all hidden from sight as Roundtree approached the train. He looked up at Raider and then he realized that Escobar was standing beside him. Roundtree, a fat man, reined back so hard that his bay stallion reared, almost throwing him out of the saddle.

Escobar raised the rifle. "I want my herd back, Roundtree."

A saggy, bulldog face snarled at them. "These ain't yours."

"Wouldn't want us to check the brand, would you?" Raider asked.

Rifle levers chinked behind the fat man.

Roundtree raised his hand. "No! No gunfire. These cattle will run if you . . . Oh my God, no."

His eyes had lifted to the boxcar again.

Raider stood on the roof, holding a stick of dynamite in his hand. He lit the short fuse and held the red shaft out toward Roundtree. Raider grinned and looked back toward the herd.

"Are you loco?" Roundtree cried.

Raider nodded toward the hired guns behind their boss. They were all drawn, hands full. "Tell them boys to drop it slow-like."

"He's bluffing."

The voice had come from the kid with the white Stetson. Raider studied Johnny Dallas, the fuse dripping sparks. "Try me, boy," he replied.

Johnny Dallas rode forward a little. "Go on. Let's see you throw it."

Raider glanced at Escobar. "I guess it's gonna come down to it."

He drew back like he was going to throw the dynamite at Roundtree's feet. The fat man's face contracted in a hateful scowl. He cried out, causing Raider to stop the forward motion of his arm.

Roundtree held up his hand. "Drop 'em," he hollered. "Just like the man said. Go on. You too, Dallas."

Their guns hit the ground. Immediately Escobar's men came out of the train where they had been hiding. Some held rifles on Roundtree's men while the others gathered up the iron.

Raider flashed back at Johnny Dallas. The kid still had his gun in his holster, his hand twitching over the gun butt. Slitted eyes fixed on the burning fuse of the red stick in Raider's hand.

The big Pinkerton held out the dynamite toward the kid.

"How about it, Dallas? Are you gonna make all of these people hate you by makin' me throw this hot potato?"

The fuse had almost burned into the shiny percussion cap.

Johnny Dallas cried, "They hate me already! Ever'body hates me!"

The kid's hand dropped for his gun. Escobar fired the silver-plated Winchester but he missed Johnny Dallas. The kid let off one burst that whizzed over Miguel's shoulder.

Raider's reflexes had taken over. He had to ditch the hot dynamite. Drawing back again, he tossed the red shaft into the air, flinging it far behind Roundtree and his men. Raider cried for everyone to hit the dirt.

The explosion went off over their heads. Raider felt the concussion in his entire body. His ears were ringing when he looked up.

Roundtree and his men had been knocked off their horses.

The screaming cattle were running in all directions, trampling most of the fallen men. Escobar's men had dived under the train, escaping the raging hooves. Raider watched the spectacle, looking for Johnny Dallas. Had the kid been trampled like the others?

The herd split in two directions, slowing as it moved farther away from the train.

Escobar came next to the big man, staring at his scrambled herd. "Did you have to do that, gringo? Look at them."

"The name's Raider," the big man replied. "And you can put a cork in it, Miguel. I got your herd back, didn't I?"

His black eyes flashed at Raider. "Yes, and you almost killed us in the bargain."

Raider gestured toward the bodies that were strewn on the plain. "Tell Roundtree. If you can find him."

Suddenly Miguel rattled the level of the Winchester.

Raider reached for his Colt.

They drew down. Raider thumbed the hammer of the Colt. Sweat beads broke on Miguel's forehead.

They remained still for a moment.

"Are we gonna do it?" Raider asked.

Miguel smiled. Then he laughed. "I just wanted to see how fast you were, grin . . . Raider."

Raider tried not to laugh, but after a few seconds he couldn't contain himself.

* * *

Escobar was nice enough to help Raider clear things up. They made official reports with the Texas Rangers and then went back to Flat Rock to tell the judge that he wouldn't be having any more trouble with Roundtree. The judge said he would notify Roundtree's next of kin, if they could be found. He'd declare Roundtree's spread open to homesteaders again.

Raider would not accept a reward, but he asked that it be given to Preacher Newton and his young daughter for the church. Raider hadn't been to church in a long time and he figured he owed something.

When all that was finished, he rode south again to pick up the train to Austin.

In the Texas state capital, Raider rested for a day and then picked up his prisoner, a man named Harley Louder, a weak-faced sort that was wanted in Kansas City for killing a woman. Raider bound and gagged him and stuck him in the mail car. He didn't want any trouble on the trip north.

In spite of the smooth transition, Raider couldn't help but feel that something wasn't finished. His guts were churning. A damned hunch. He tried to shake off the jitters, but when it wouldn't leave, he just chalked it up to being so late and his fear of reprisal from Allan Pinkerton.

So the train chugged on into the night. On one of the stops for water and wood, Raider climbed down out of the train and went forth into a small town, looking for a drink. He found a slug of homemade red-eye in a drape-doored cantina that stirred with a hot wind from the Texas plain. The few barflies were friendly until the cloth door parted and a palm of warm air blew through the dim yellow enclosure.

Raider saw the barflies scatter.

A high-pitched voice sounded behind him. "Well, if it ain't the dynamite man."

As he turned, the big man recognized the white Stetson.

He faced the kid head-on. "Johnny Dallas. How the hell are you, boy?"

The slitted eyes could have belonged to a rattlesnake. "I just came from humpin' your mother, big man. What do you think of that?"

Raider straightened his body. "I'm thinkin' you want to try me. Otherwise you would have shot me in the back already."

Johnny Dallas shivered. His face was white, covered with kid-fuzz. Eyes like cold flint.

It was like a grizzly and a cougar facing off.

Raider didn't see the need for a fight. "Let it ride, Johnny Dallas. You were a hired man back there in Texas. I ain't got nothin' agin you personal-like. How the hell did you get out of there anyway?"

But Johnny Dallas wasn't in a mood for talking. "I got to take you, big man. You made a fool out of me."

Raider's black eyes came up under the brim of his hat. "Then we finish it. Now!"

Raider dived forward as Johnny Dallas flashed his Colt. The slug flew over the big man from Arkansas, thudding in the planked wall behind him. Raider's Peacemaker exploded twice, chopping chunks out of the kid's forehead. Raider crashed through a flimsy table, hitting the dirt floor.

Dallas stumbled forward, blood surging from the hole in his brow. He looked down at Raider, trying to point his Colt. Raider had to fire again, knocking the kid backward before he got off a last-ditch lucky shot.

The trainmen ran in as Raider regained his feet. They looked down at Johnny Dallas whose body had stopped moving. The engineer asked the cantina owner if there was a lawman nearabouts. The cantina proprietor replied that there was no sheriff, but that he would be glad to bury the body as Johnny Dallas was a source of aggravation to all the neighboring territories. He was glad Raider had killed the kid. Dallas had needed killing.

The barflies echoed the cantina owner's sentiments.

Raider decided not to write a report on the incident. The trainmen said they wouldn't mention the killing to anyone, seeing as how it was justified. All were in agreement that the whole thing was best forgotten.

"It's finished," Raider said.

And he knew it was, because the nagging feeling had left him.

CHAPTER SIX

Raider thought Kansas City was like all overgrown towns west of the Mississippi—it had a certain smell to it that was unmistakable. It stunk of cattle pens, smokestacks, cluttered streets, and cheap saloons. A man couldn't rightly find a breath of fresh air if he had a hundred bucks and a new nose. Still, there were other things that a city offered, and Raider took to these with a vengeance—women, gambling, and whiskey, mainly.

Raider knew that there would be a message waiting for him when he got off the train in K.C. Allan Pinkerton himself had sent a wire directing him to *Disregard all previous orders to wait for my arrival*. The dispatch did not give an estimated time of arrival, which put the big man in limbo while he waited for his boss.

Damn. Pinkerton was coming himself. That always meant something big was hatching. It called for caution all the way around. Best to stay out of trouble. The prisoner was safe and sound in jail. Nothing to do but wait.

The telegram directed him to the Sundowner Hotel. A fine place. Not what Raider would have picked, but classy enough for the big boss. Raider could not help but wonder if Pinkerton was mad at him. He was damned late.

It wouldn't do any good to worry. Did Pinkerton know

about the mess in Flat Rock? Best to stay quiet. Raider sought to content himself with the simple pleasures to cure his trail weariness. Things like food and drink and a hot bath. Best to stay away from women, what with the big chief on the way. The boss. The only man Raider hated to face.

But darkness came on and Raider felt the call into the city's darker regions, where a man could scare up the necessities beyond the creature comforts—a losing round of poker, a bottle of good Irish whiskey, the smoky joy of a gambling parlor, the inevitable buxom barmaid who could not tear herself away from the tall man's black eyes. He could not resist that healthy cleavage, especially after she smiled back. When the evening was nearing an end, Raider found himself leaning against the bar, ordering another drink just to be near her.

Her red lips curled in a playful smirk. "Bar's closin', cowpoke. Best be headin' back to whatever barn you're sleepin' in."

Raider grinned, dropping the hotel key in front of her. "Don't get that at a barn." He fought the urge to reach out to touch her coarse black hair.

Soft brown eyes conceded his one-upmanship. "Didn't figure you for no fancy-pants. Maybe I will let you have one more drink."

As she filled his shot glass, Raider knew it was going to happen. She wouldn't come right out and say it, because women never came right out to say it. They had to have the playacting, the bedroom drama, stringing it out, pretending it wasn't going to be, so when it did happen, it was all the more exciting.

"So, fancy man," she said, "how long you in town for?"

Raider shrugged. "Can't say. S'posed to meet my boss here, but he ain't showed yet. When he comes, could ship out any minute."

She raised a thick eyebrow. "You a boatman?"

He shook his head. "No. Name's Raider. Some say I'm what you'd call a troublemaker. Others call me a detective."

She leaned forward on the bar, making sure he caught the vertical line of her bosom. "What in creation is a detective?"

"I take on other people's trouble," Raider replied. "I solve things. All by my lonesome."

She smiled a little. "Bet you've seen a few things."

"If you only knew," Raider chortled.

There was a disquieting lull in the conversation. For a moment, Raider thought he had lost her. She moved down the bar to collect the last money from a couple of boys who wanted a bottle to take with them. But then she came back, leaning on the counter again.

Raider cleared his throat, gazing into her dark eyes. She had a round face and a body to match. He liked them big. Skinny women had too many bones to poke and jab you.

"You gettin' off work soon?" he asked.

She shrugged. "Maybe."

"Rough parts around here. Maybe you need somebody to walk you home."

"Home to my husband," she said bluntly.

Raider frowned. "Er, sorry, honey."

"Name's Lottie."

"Yeah, well, I reckon I better be goin', Lottie."

As he tried to pull away from the bar, Lottie grabbed his hand. "My husband is lying drunk somewhere. He ain't walked me home in over a year."

Raider still had his doubts. "Is he the kind that might want to shoot anybody who's walkin' with you?"

She shook her head and smiled. "Doesn't even own a gun."

Raider's brow fretted. "I ain't much on spendin' time with a woman who's hitched."

Her hand was warm on his skin. "Just to walk me home. What harm would there be in that?"

Raider nodded, even though he knew that she wasn't really talking about the walk home. He waited for her to clean up, and then they exited the gaming house by a side door. A man with a pistol under his coat bade them good night and closed the door behind them.

As soon as they were in the dark alley, Lottie grabbed Raider and pressed her lips to his mouth. For a minute, he thought she was going to suck out his tongue. She grinded her crotch against his, pressing her large breasts into his body. He cupped her nipples and felt them tighten under his palms. Her entire body shivered when she reached down for the lump in his pants.

"God, cowboy, you're so handsome. I knew it the second I saw you. I wanted you. I never want men who come in to my place, but I wanted you."

Raider had to catch his breath. "We can't do it right here in the alley. And I ain't goin' to your place."

She reached into his vest pocket and took out the room key. "You got that fancy hotel waiting."

"Let's get the hell out of here."

He ushered her toward the main street. As luck would have it, a carriage for hire, one of the city's few liveries, was passing by on its way to a livery barn. Raider tossed the driver a silver dollar and gave him the name of the hotel.

Raider and Lottie touched and kissed all the way back to the hotel, where Raider tipped the driver another dollar.

At the main entrance, Raider hesitated.

Lottie knew what he was thinking. "Can't exactly take me in through the front gate, eh."

"They kinda frown on unmarried ladies and gents mixin' it up under their roof," he replied.

"You forget," she teased. "I'm married."

Raider felt the aching in his groin. "How are we gonna work this?"

She took his hand. "For a dee-tective, you sure ain't smart as you ought to be."

"I ain't exactly thinkin' straight right now."

"There's always the back entrance. Hell, I ain't proud."

She surely wasn't. With a frightening stealth, Lottie led Raider to the back door. They found their way up a flight of unused stairs and emerged into the hallway of Raider's floor.

Lottie gave him a big kiss and then said, "Maybe I ought to become a dee-tective myself."

Raider fumbled with the key. "Let's get out of this hallway before—"

"It's about time you showed your face, Raider!"

The voice boomed down the corridor. Raider did not have to turn to see who it was. He knew the unmistakable baritone of his boss, Allan Pinkerton. Lottie was also frozen by his side, peering with wide eyes at the towering man who strode down the hall. Pinkerton sauntered toward them, frowning like a buzzard with a bellyache.

Raider stepped back away from the door. "Er, I was just helpin' this lady with the lock on this room. She, uh, that is . . ."

With a gentlemanly grace that caught Raider off guard, Pinkerton took Lottie's hand and bowed from the waist. "Good evening," he said formally, "I do hate to deprive you of Mr. Raider's company, but unfortunately he had a previous business meeting." He smiled warmly. "You see, I am Raider's supervisor, and I just arrived from Chicago to see him. I'm sure you understand that I have come a long way. So, if you will excuse us."

Lottie smiled bashfully. "Well land sakes, but you do know how to talk to a girl. Are you a dee-tective too?"

Pinkerton sniffed and straightened his huge frame. "Quite." He gave an accusing, sidelong glance to Raider. "Immediately, Raider."

As he strode off down the hall, Lottie giggled.

"It ain't funny," the big man replied.

She kissed his cheek. "All in all, you better go."

"He's gonna skin my worthless hide!"

Lottie patted his cheek. "He seemed sweet to me."

"Uh-huh."

She gave a little curtsy. "My, my, if it ain't a pleasure to meet two fine gentlemen in one night."

Raider was hurting between his thighs. "Lottie, I know this didn't work out like we woulda wanted, but—"

She put her fingers on his lips. "Just go on, honey, and don't worry about it. We'll see each other again. I promise."

Raider drew a sorrowful breath. "Yeah."

He followed Pinkerton down the hall.

Allan Pinkerton was officious with his lecture to Raider. He went on about the dignity of his agents, the need for good moral conduct, and the necessity of staying within the lines of duty. Raider took it all with the growing impatience of a man who does not like to be dressed down by anyone, even the man who payed his wages.

The big man's face grew redder, the crimson hue of anger spreading all the way to his ears. Pinkerton was driving in the nails, one by one. Raider was set to explode like the red stick of dynamite that had scattered a herd of cows in Texas.

"And furthermore," Pinkerton railed, "as you know, I usually do not venture into the field myself unless there is a case that has a personal relation to me."

Raider nodded, trying to mutter in agreement, his eyes cast down on his boots. He figured he had to take it from someone. Everybody had somebody over them in life. That was the way it worked out. You just had to take it.

Pinkerton did not let up. "And what do I find when I arrive? First, that you are not waiting for me, and secondly, that you are in the company of a woman whose reputation at best—"

"She needed help," Raider replied, bristling. "Sometimes you just got to lend folks a helpin' hand."

Pinkerton's eyes narrowed. He stopped pacing back and forth. His gaze made Raider's spine tingle. "A helping hand, you say?" He picked up a sheaf of papers. "Like the helping hand you gave to Judge Farnsworth in New Mexico? Or was that Texas where you almost single-handedly started a range war?"

Raider slunk down in the chair with a defeated half smile on his face. "Beggin' your pardon, Mr. Pinkerton, but I believe that I single-handedly stopped a range war from happenin'."

Pinkerton pointed a finger at him. "You deliberately went out of your way to stir up trouble. You acted on your own."

"Didn't nobody else want to help that judge," Raider said in his own defense. "He was suckin' hind tit, Mr. Pinkerton."

"None of your colorful metaphors," his boss warned.

As Pinkerton began pacing again, Raider tried to think of other lines of work he could do. The big man sighed. He didn't want to listen to any more bad-mouthing. As far as he could see, he was getting the job done. What more could Pinkerton ask?

Raider stood up.

Pinkerton eyed him. "Where do you think you're going?"

Raider shrugged. "I reckon I'm gonna find me another job," he replied. "Don't seem like you're too set on me stayin' on. I reckon I do have to admire the way you found out about that business in Flat Rock. I couldn't help it though. The judge was backed up to the wall."

"Sit down," Pinkerton grumbled. He threw Raider an envelope full of money. "Your back pay."

"You mean I ain't fired?" Raider said, sitting back in the chair.

"No," Pinkerton muttered. "But you would have been if it weren't for that commendation from the territorial governor's office. New Mexico appreciated your efforts far more than I did. The Texas Rangers speak highly of you as well."

Raider smiled a little. "A commendation, huh. I got me a commendation."

"Don't get cocky," the head man warned. "We have real business to attend to. Don't forget that."

Raider shook his head. A commendation. That hadn't happened in a long time. A lucky sign. A damned commendation!

Pinkerton reined back, letting go of the venom he had been spewing. He could do that sometimes, Raider thought. Change directions in midstream. A brilliant man with a head for pointedness and accuracy. After a moment, he resumed his discourse.

"Have you ever heard of a man named Jake Kelsey?"

Raider's brow wrinkled. He was studying the problem with the expertise of a man with a commendation. "Can't say that I have. Unless you mean ole Cougar Kelsey. He was a gunfighter."

Pinkerton nodded his approval at the big man. "Precisely who I mean. What do you know about him?"

Raider shrugged. "I heard he was dead. Been around for the longest time before that. Used to be a gunfighter. Not one of the big names, but he did make a reputation for himself by beatin' a boy name of Wade Turner, around Lampasas, I think. Rode that reputation until he finally just give out, as far as I know. Somebody said he was killed in the Indian wars."

Pinkerton shook his head. "No, I'm afraid not. 'Cougar' Jake Kelsey is still alive and well, even though he's nearing his sixth decade in age."

"Huh?" Raider grunted.

"He's almost sixty," Pinkerton explained.

"Oh. Well, I reckon he ain't totin' a gun," Raider said.

"Wrong again," Pinkerton replied. "He's making his living

with a gun. Or at least he plans to."

"Come again?"

Pinkerton reached into his traveling valise and pulled out a tube of rolled paper. He spread out a poster that was done in red, white, and blue. The poster declaimed: "Henry Masters Presents the Six-gun Circus. Extravaganza, Spectacle, and Thrills. Wild West Excitement and Circus Show. See the one and only 'Cougar' Jake Kelsey. World's Oldest Living Gunfighter."

Below the large print, in smaller letters: "Hear Ramona Masters, the Georgia Nightingale."

Raider examined the poster carefully, remarking that there were no dates or times for the extravaganza. Raider wondered what it had to do with him. He had no desire to see a circus.

Pinkerton hastily rolled up the poster. "The point is this, Raider. Henry Masters is the brother of Simon Masters, a very old and dear friend of mine who has since departed this world. When Simon died, he asked that I look out for his younger brother. He never approved of Henry's foray into the world of showmanship, not that I've had to do that much watching over Henry. He's done quite well for himself, except of late."

"Of late?" Raider asked. "You mean recent-like?"

Pinkerton snorted. "Yes, he's fallen on rather hard times. For the longest period he had his circus touring the East, as well as the Midwest. But he's been spending large sums of money promoting his young wife's singing."

Raider gestured to the poster. "Ramona? The Georgia Nightingale?"

Pinkerton nodded. "Sometimes I almost have hopes for you, Raider. Yes, that's her. I met her once. A lovely young thing. Henry Masters is quite taken with her. And she has a tolerable voice."

Raider's face slacked. "Just tolerable, huh? You make that sound like a bad thing."

"I'm no judge of music," Pinkerton said blankly. "I just hate to see an older man lose his head over a pretty face."

Raider's eyes narrowed. "So what's all this got to do with Cougar Kelsey and the Wild West show?"

Pinkerton threw out his hands. "Masters and Kelsey are teaming up to form a Wild West and circus show, with the idea of touring the West. Kelsey's arranging for the riders and trick shoot artists; in the meantime, Masters is donating the remains of his bankrupt circus."

Raider smiled. "And together, they've come up with the Six-gun Circus. Not bad."

Pinkerton nodded. "I have to admit that it's catchy. Although I tend to doubt the draw of a show that features action seen every day west of the Mississippi. Henry plans to tour the western territories. It could fail miserably."

Raider nodded. "Maybe, but you know how it can be. Sometimes a man'll walk fifty miles just to see a hangin'. Why not pay a few cents to see a show that's comin' to you?"

Pinkerton thought Raider had a good point.

Only then did the big man ask the most obvious question. "Why am I bein' called in on this thing, Mr. Pinkerton?"

"Protection," his boss replied. "There's been trouble already with the show, and it's still just forming."

"What kind of trouble?"

"Two things. One, the theft of a large strongbox full of gold—five thousand dollars, to be exact. And, more importantly, an attempt on Jake Kelsey's life."

Raider blurted out, "Somebody tried to kill the star of the show?"

"I don't know the details," Pinkerton replied, "but that's your job to find out. The show is quartered over behind the cattle yard. You will have the dubious honor of protecting Jake Kelsey. Raider, what are you smiling about?"

The big man shrugged. "Just seems kinda funny, me guardin' the man who killed Wade Turner. Even if he is an old geezer."

Pinkerton flushed red, obviously losing patience with Raider's impertinence. "Geezer or not, you will do everything you can to secure his well-being. Report first thing tomorrow morning. Is that understood?"

Raider nodded. "Understood."

"Now get out of here and stay out of trouble."

"I promise there won't be any commotion, sir," the big man said.

Pinkerton scowled cynically at his best detective. "Of course not."

"I mean it, sir. I really do."

And Raider did mean it, at least until he got back to his room.

"See, Raider, I told you we'd see each other again."

The big man had just stepped into his room and closed the door behind him.

"Are you loco, woman?"

Lottie was lying in his bed, under the covers. "You left the room key with me, remember?"

Raider wondered if he might just be pushing his luck. "You can't stay here, not with my boss down the hall." He snuck a quick peek out of the door and then slammed it tight again.

Lottie kept right on smiling. "Aw, he ain't gonna hear us." She licked her lips. "Though you look like you might stir up a ruckus. Want to stir up a ruckus, cowboy?"

Raider unhitched his gunbelt and hung it on the end of the bed. "Only thing I'm want to stir up is some sleep. I got a big day ahead of me tomorrow. And what with Mr. Pinkerton... Whoa... Lottie!"

She had thrown back the covers, revealing her voluptuous body. Her thick thighs were parted, her breasts falling to both sides. Raider just stood there gawking at her.

"Still want me to leave?" she asked.

"I... aw..."

She put her hands behind her head, flexing her arms to make her breasts rise slightly. "I had time to take a bath and get all sweet-smelling for you. I can't believe that you'd let me go."

Raider's better nature gave way to the trail-weary saddle bum who had not been in a real bed with a willing woman in over a month. The preacher's daughter hadn't been like this, Raider thought. He caught the scent of her body. Where had she found the perfume?

"Get into bed, Raider. If you want to get some sleep, we'd better start now."

He dropped his shirt and his pants on the floor, sliding in next to her on the smooth sheets. The feather mattress sagged with their combined weights. Lottie pulled the covers over them.

"Good evening, Mr. Raider."

He caught on to her act. "Why, pleased to make your acquaintance, Miss Lottie. You are lookin' a mite pretty today."

"Oh, I just love a gentleman."

Her hands rubbed his chest, working over the scars from a thousand battles. Following her natural inclination, she asked him about every one, forcing Raider to recount each tale from beginning to end. She patted his tight stomach and then reached between his thighs.

Lottie tossed back the covers again to examine him more closely. "Umm, cowboy, when God was handin' out whangers, you musta been standin' in line with the horses."

Raider started to roll over on top of her, but she stopped him. "What's wrong with you?" he asked.

"Nothin'. I just want to take my time. There's somethin' I been wantin' to try. You ever have a woman . . . you know . . ."

Her lips puckered in and out.

Raider groaned. "Where'd you hear about stuff like that?"

She shrugged, becoming slightly indignant. "I heard. I had me this Frenchy girl workin' for me a while back. She said they did that kinda thing all the time in France. Men do it to women, too." She smiled and cocked her head sideways. "You ever do it, cowboy?"

Raider blushed. "Maybe."

"Oh. Then you won't mind . . ."

He never had minded. Although he still thought it wasn't something right to do. Her mouth was sinful on him. He closed his eyes and let her have her way.

When her curiosity had been appeased, Lottie looked up again and grinned at him. "You like it?"

Raider only nodded.

"Now you do it to me."

"No!"

Her lower lip protruded. "But you said you had."

"I ain't in the mood."

She threw herself back on the pillows, folding her arms.

Raider touched her cheek with his fingertips. "Hey, don't be like that. Hell, we can get you goin'. Let me see . . ."

She protested a little until his lips fell on her shoulders. Lottie moaned and told him how good if felt. Raider kissed her neck too, biting softly in the right places.

Lottie's arms unfolded. Raider took her breasts in his hands, lifting them to his mouth. His mustache tickled the silver-dollar pink circles of her nipples.

"Touch me there, cowboy," she whispered.

Raider stroked the insides of her thighs. The wet trickle had spilled onto her white skin. He used a finger to find the sensitive folds of her cunt, triggering a volcanic reaction in Lottie's round body.

Her hand closed around his massive prick, jerking him violently. Lottie spread out, grabbing Raider's shoulders to pull him on top of her. The big man from Arkansas complied, settling in between her legs.

"That thing is so big," she whined.

Raider slipped himself into position. "Yeah, but I think you can take it all."

Lottie cried out when he gave her the entire length with one savage thrust. Her expression of agony eased into a tortured smile. Her tongue came out of her mouth, rolling around on her lips.

"Slooow," she moaned.

Raider tried to go slow for a while, but it didn't work. The longer he stayed inside her, the more he felt compelled to hasten the motion of his hips. Lottie gripped the cheeks of his ass, trying to control his powerful plunges.

"Oh God, oh cowboy. . ."

"Shh."

Raider started to find his rhythm, thrusting his cock in and out of her. Lottie was cooperative, but the bed wasn't. The mattress sagged, making it impossible for Raider to complete his climax. They were bumping off the damned floor.

"Oh no," Lottie said. "Don't stop!"

Raider pulled out of her and rolled off the bed.

"What are you doin', cowboy?"

Raider snatched a sheet off the bed and spread it out on the floor. "Get down here, woman."

Lottie smiled. "Oh, I see. Yes, I do."

She joined him, spreading out on her back, eager to have him inside her once again. "Now don't you stop."

Raider got a funny look in his eyes. Lottie had brought out something inside him. A nasty side that he had cultivated in the bedrooms of whores, saloon gals, Indian and foreign women, wives and sisters, proper women and gypsies.

Lottie noticed his curious expression. "What?"

"Nothin'."

Raider settled in between her legs again, fitting his cock into her tight crevice. He humped her again for a long time, but he did not release. Lottie, on the other hand, had climaxed more times than he could count. She held his face, looking up into his eyes.

"Raider, you okay?"

He nodded. "Yeah, it's just that I was thinkin' about somethin' I done before with women. Now I got it on my mind and I can't think about nothin' else. You know what I mean?"

She smiled wickedly. "Let's do it."

Raider had a concerned gleam in his eyes. "Are you sure?"

"I want to. I really do."

"Okay."

He pulled out of her and got up on his knees.

Lottie had an eager look on her face. "What do I do?"

"Get up on all fours. You know, the way animals do it."

Raider expected some protest or doubts, but Lottie played the willing pupil. When she was ready, he slid behind her and penetrated her to the hilt of his prick. Lottie sighed, on her way to yet another release.

Raider shook her quivering body, nearing his own climax. When he came, Lottie collapsed on the floor. Raider fell on top of her, grinding until he was completely spent.

Lottie turned over, pressing her breasts against his chest, kissing him all over his face and neck. "I'll never forget this night, cowboy."

"Maybe we oughta get back in bed and get some sleep."

But when they were back in bed, Lottie managed to renew Raider's interest in her. Again they had to climb onto the floor to complete a second coupling, with Raider climaxing on top. They slid onto the mattress for the last time, both of them falling off to sleep in a matter of minutes.

Raider awoke in the middle of the night to find that Lottie was no longer in bed with him. He would have drifted back into slumber without a second thought, if not for the commotion outside his door in the hallway. The big man found his Colt and stepped to the threshold.

A man and a woman were arguing outside in the corridor.

Raider cracked the door enough to hear a man's pleading voice. He was trying to keep a woman out of his room.

"My good woman," he was saying, "this is highly irregular. I don't appreciate your waking me—"

"I just want to come in for a little while," she said. "You're such a fine gentleman. I just want to—"

"Raider! Get out here."

The voice had come from the direction of Allan Pinkerton's room.

The big man slipped on his pants and eased out into the hall. Lottie was standing at the door of Allan Pinkerton's room. Raider feigned ignorance, playing the innocent bystander, the wide-eyed witness.

"Sorry, Mr. Pinkerton." Raider gawked bashfully. "I didn't mean to bust in on any fun you might be havin'."

Pinkerton turned as red as a Gila monster's stripes. "This woman awoke me in the middle of the night." He pointed a finger at his most violent operative. "And you put her up to this, Raider!"

The big man from Arkansas grinned sheepishly. "Me?"

Lottie pressed herself against Pinkerton. "No, it was my idea, sir. I don't even know this man." She smirked at Raider. "Why, do you think I would lower myself to be with a man like him?"

Pinkerton nodded, pushing her away. "I see what you mean. But you must go now. Raider! Escort this woman to her room."

"Yes, sir."

Lottie moved toward the big man.

Pinkerton started back into his room.

"Sir," Raider said, stopping him. "This will be 'twixt us gents, if you know what I mean. It won't go no further."

Pinkerton stormed into his room and slammed the door.

Raider glared at Lottie.

"Sorry," she said. "I just . . ."

Raider whisked her back to his room. He had almost been in a sinkhole back there. How much longer would Pinkerton put up with him walkin' the line?

When they were in his bedroom, Lottie grimaced at him. "Are you mad at me?"

Raider smiled and shrugged. "Nah. It was kinda funny."

"You don't think I'm a bad woman?"

"I think your britches is hot," he replied. "Only you was barkin' up the wrong tree with ole Pinkerton there."

Lottie started to get out of her clothes again. "What's the matter? Don't he like women?"

"Yeah," Raider replied. "Only he likes a certain kind of woman. Fancy and all refined. He's more the kind to be a family man."

Lottie tossed her skirt on the floor.

"What are you doin'?" Raider asked, gawking at her brushy wedge.

"Well," she replied, "I figured as long as I was here . . ."

When she touched him, he slowly sprang back to life.

Raider wasn't really in the mood, but he knew if he didn't do it that he would think about it on the trail. He'd remember that she wanted to and he didn't. And after a long time between women, he'd wish that he had done it then, when it was ready and available.

It could be a long time between women on the trail.

So they stretched out on the floor again, but this time they did not return to the bed when they were ready to sleep.

CHAPTER SEVEN

The next morning, Allan Pinkerton said his farewells and hightailed it back to Chicago. When he was gone, Raider used his back pay to purchase a fresh gray gelding. As he plodded toward the stockyards where the circus was encamped, he considered his relationship with Pinkerton.

His boss, like Raider's ex-partner, was a gentleman. He tried to do the right thing all the time. Raider wanted to follow suit, but he knew better than to think a man could always do right. The big man from Arkansas walked the wide gray line, the territory between right and wrong, where men with guns decided things the hard way. When you got down to it, right and wrong often appeared to be the same thing unless you looked real close.

The big man shifted in his saddle, straightening his body. Sometimes the bones reminded him that he wasn't twenty years old anymore. He was still quick, but not the fastest. When his speed failed him, he had to use smarts. Years of learning on each new case. Doc had taught him a lot. Now that Doc was gone, he had to be that much smarter. It made him keen, but it wore him out too.

He wondered if Pinkerton really trusted him. The head man and Wagner did their best to ration out the shit. They complained about his brief, poorly penned reports, his lack of depositions from the witnesses at killings, the number of bodies reported by the territorial marshals. But for all his fretting, Pinkerton had chosen Raider for a mission of personal importance. Even if he didn't trust the big man, the boss knew he could get the job done.

Raider looked up. He heard pounding hammers in the distance. The circus camp rose up in front of him like a scurrying mass of men and women running around on a Mexican red anthill. Hundreds of tents and wagons housed the troupe.

"Looks like the Six-gun Circus done come to town."

He spurred the gray and bolted into the encampment.

Raider climbed off the gray at the edge of the circus grounds. He led the horse through the crowd of performers and stagehands, all geared to various activities. Wagons and tents were set up at lengthy intervals, with each act engaged in intense rehearsal. Raider counted clowns, acrobats, cowboys twirling ropes, a strongman, the bearded lady, dwarfs, giants, roustabouts, more cowboys, and a score of shapely, good-looking women.

No one paid much attention to Raider, so he moved freely among them. He felt uplifted at the sight of so many people involved in different, exciting chores. Show folk. They were different, all right. He had encountered them before, but never in such numbers—a woman with snakes, the smallest man west of the Mississippi, the fire-eater, a man with tattoos all over his body.

"You there!"

A freakish face loomed out at Raider from the back of a circus box wagon—an older man with a pointed beard and a gray mustache. The old fellow's eyes were spooky-looking. He furled a black cape around his shoulders and pointed at Raider.

"You," he said. "You have come into danger. All around you." He spread the cape with an encompassing gesture. "And you will die."

Raider almost drew down on the wrinkled old buzzard.

"The cards tell all," the man said, flashing something with a picture of the Grim Reaper on it. "You are chosen. I have seen it all."

"You been eatin' funny cactus, old-timer?"

"My name is Excalibur, Professor Excalibur. I am a seer, a soothsayer, a teller of fortunes. I also delve into the art of common magic, to make a meager wage with this dilapidated carnival that Mr. Masters laughingly calls a circus."

Raider thought he saw the first chance to glean some information. "You sayin' you don't like it here?"

Excalibur wrapped the cape around his body, looking warily in both directions. "Where else would I go? A man of my talents. I must stay here until . . . until the end."

"You make it sound like this circus is in trouble," Raider offered.

Excaliur began to back away. "Trouble? Nay, I know not trouble. Unless trouble is spelled d-o-o-m. Ha. Ha-ha." He began to laugh maniacally.

Raider squinted at Professor Excalibur, not quite knowing what to believe. He suddenly felt something on his calf. Someone tugging at his pants leg. He looked down at a dwarf, a man no taller than three feet.

"Hello there, little feller.

The dwarf frowned at him. "My name's not Little Feller. It's Augie. Augie Sanders. And I'm the shortest man west of the Mississippi."

Raider tipped his hat. "Fair enough. My name's Raider. I'm lookin' for your boss, a Mr. Henry Masters."

Augie eyed him knowingly. "The Pinkerton, I'll bet. You were sent to guard the show."

Raider smiled and nodded. "Smart boy."

"I'm not a boy, I'm a man. I'll bet I'm older than you. I'm forty-one years old."

"Older than me," Raider conceded. "Course you don't look a day over seven. Not from up here, anyway."

Augie hesitated for a second before he started to laugh. Raider chuckled as well. Augie gestured with his hand. "Come on, I'll take you to Mr. Ma . . . What are you doing?"

Raider had grabbed Augie's shoulder. He had also drawn his Colt. He gawked at the little man. "Didn't you hear it? There, again. Gunshots."

"From over there," Augie replied. "But you don't have . . ."

Raider broke into a full run, pushing through the circus

people. The shots continued to ring out, coming from a corral, Raider figured. A crowd had gathered at the fence to watch something. A gunfight? he wondered. Sometimes the police would look the other way if two gents took their fight outside the city limits.

The big man crashed through the spectators and pulled himself up on the railing. Another pistol shot exploded. Something shattered in the air. The crowd applauded a man on horseback. He rode the length of the corral, turning full tilt as something was launched overhead. The man drew his iron again and fired at the object, smashing it into a thousand pieces. Again the audience erupted in cheers and handclaps.

Raider quickly holstered his Colt and continued to watch the trick-shoot artist. He had to be Jake Kelsey. His silver hair flowed out of his white Stetson, shoulder length like Custer's. He had a cream-colored buckskin jacket and light-colored buckskin pants with mirrors down the sides, a dark shirt, and a gold bandanna around his neck. He could still ride, Raider thought. It had also been a long time since the big man had seen such fancy shooting.

"Cougar" Jake Kelsey stopped the palomino gelding in the center of the corral. He raised his feet and then stood on the saddle. His hands hovered over the twin Colts that hung in the pearl-encrusted holsters that went with the rest of his outfit.

"Two!" he cried in a cracking voice.

Raider thought the objects were goards hurling through the air. Cougar Kelsey slapped leather and brought up both shooting irons. The gourds shattered at the same time. Raider found himself applauding with the rest of the onlookers. Cougar was still good.

Why did they call him Cougar? Raider seemed to remember that the old gent, in his younger days, had strangled a cougar with his bare hands. That was impossible, Raider figured, but the story still had a certain attraction around the campfire.

Kelsey sat back down on the saddle and waved his white hat. "That's all for today, folks."

As the audience began to disperse, Augie came up next to Raider.

"He's pretty good with them six-guns," Raider said.

"If you mean that he could shoot the ass out of a lightning bug, you're damned straight," Augie replied. "Cougar Jake is the best ever!"

Raider smiled. "Careful, Augie. Things ain't always what they seem."

The little man shook his head. "You been talkin' to that loco fortune-teller?"

Raider ignored the little man, tipping his hat to Jake Kelsey as he guided the palomino next to the fence.

Kelsey's gray-ringed eyes glared down at them. "Show's over for today, greenhorns."

Raider grinned at the aged cowboy. "Hell, pardner, I'm here on business. That was some pretty fancy shootin', though."

Raider withdrew his credentials from his vest pocket. He showed them to Kelsey and explained that he had been sent by Allan Pinkerton to lend a hand protecting the circus. An extra gun in case there was more trouble.

Kelsey nodded. "Pinkerton, eh?" He slapped his holsters. "Only protection I need is right here."

"And you sure as hell know you to use 'em," Raider replied. "How about letting me see some of that fancy shootin' again?"

Kelsey looked a little puzzled until Raider added, "A man in my line of work can always use a few pointers when it comes to shootin'."

Kelsey shrugged. Raider thought he could see the years etched in his tanned hide. Gunfighters rarely made it to a ripe old age. There was always somebody around, usually a kid, with a faster gunhand. Kelsey had been one of the lucky fossils.

"So you want shootin', do you?" He glanced to the side. "Augie! Throw up two. Clay gourds," he said to Raider. "When the show's on, they're filled with flashy pieces of paper. Look's like it's snowin' when I pop one of them. Augie, go!"

Two gourds sailed up into the air. Kelsey sighted in and drew his pistols, breaking both projectiles with a single burst from each Colt. He holstered the weapons and nodded approvingly.

"Not bad for an old 'un," the shootist boasted.

Raider shook his head admiringly. "Dead on. Hell, that horse don't even flinch."

Kelsey patted the palomino's brawny shoulder. "He was trained special by me. Never had a better horse under me in my life. I don't think I'd take ten thousand in gold for him."

Raider wore a strange expression on his face, like he had caught on to something. He swung up onto the highest rail of the corral fence, sitting with his legs over the side. Augie moved in closer, looking up at Raider, wondering what the big Pinkerton had on his mind. Raider's rugged countenance was drawn over with a fox-sly grin.

Raider patted the .45-caliber Peacemaker at his side. "You know, I'm pretty good with a pistol myself."

Cougar Jake eyed him with a patronizing smirk. "Fast are you, Tex?"

"I'm from Arkansas," Raider replied. "And I been known to draw down pretty fair in my day."

Kelsey's eyebrow raised. "Ever kill a man?"

Raider shrugged. "I scattered my share of bodies. Not that I'm proud of it. I take puttin' a man six feet under to be a serious thing. I got me a conscience, whether I want it or not. Course I never killed anyone like Wade Turner. Most of the ones I put under needed killin'. "

"Same here," Kelsey rejoined, winking at Raider. "Well, Arkansas, s'pose you tell me who you killed that I mighta knowed."

"Recent-like?" Raider asked. He thought about it, scratching his head. "Well, there was Johnny Dallas. I killed him on the way to Kansas City."

Kelsey frowned a little. "I heard of him. He's fast."

"Not fast enough. Not anymore."

Kelsey nodded approvingly. "You must be good with a gun."

"Ever hear of the California Kid?"

"Yep."

Raider nodded slightly. "I plugged him. Oklahoma Kid too."

"How do I know you're not lyin'?" Kelsey challenged.

Raider gestured toward the contraption that threw the clay

gourds up in the air for Kelsey to shoot. "Why don't I try my hand at the same thing you're doin'? Let me see how I stack up."

Kelsey laughed a little. "You're welcome to try, pardner. Augie! Git over there and throw up a couple of gourds for this Texas gunslinger."

"Arkansas," Raider said. He drew his Colt and checked the chambers to make sure he had five shots.

Kelsey guided the palomino out of the way.

Augie, who thought Raider was loco, moved over to the spring-loaded machine that tossed the gourds into the air. "You ain't gonna hit a single one," the dwarf goaded. "Nobody's as good as Jake."

Raider tipped back his hat and squared his body, his hand dangling by the butt of the Peacemaker.

"Whenever you're ready," Augie said.

Raider nodded.

Kelsey hollered, "Augie, go!"

Two projectiles flew into the air in front of Raider, who drew his Colt and fired twice. He missed the first time completely, but the second shot nicked the tip of one of the targets. Both gourds shattered on the ground, not in the air.

Kelsey nodded approvingly. "You hit one of them, not square, but you hit it. Closer than most woulda come."

Raider holstered his Peacemaker. "Guess I ain't up to your brand of shootin', Mr. Kelsey."

"Name's Jake," the old cowboy said, extending his hand.

Raider shooked the weathered paw, stepping back after a moment.

Kelsey started to urge the palomino away from him.

"Jake," Raider called.

The gray-haired shootist reined back and looked at the big Pinkerton. "Yep?"

Raider patted his holster. "You know, it seems to me that my aim has been off lately. I mean, I ain't been able to hit a bull in the butt with a handful of rice."

"Don't go blamin' yourself, big 'un," Kelsey replied.

He started off again on the horse.

Raider ran up next to him. "Oh, I ain't blamin' myself."

Kelsey reined back again. "Somethin' on your mind, boy?"

Raider kept his hand on his Colt. "It's the barrel on this damned thing. I been wonderin' if the sight is off."

"Let me look at it," Kelsey said.

Raider handed him the weapon.

Kelsey looked down the barrel and shook his head. "No, ain't a thing wrong here."

Raider took back the gun. "Well, I was wonderin' if maybe you might let me try one of your shootin' irons?"

Raider saw the not-so-subtle change in Kelsey's weathered face. He clearly did not want the big man using his show guns. But Raider persisted, finally persuading the old gunfighter to hand over one of his Colts. The scowl on Kelsey's thin mouth made it clear that he wasn't happy about Raider wielding the pistol.

Raider stepped back and squared his shoulders. "Set up two more, Augie."

"Ain't but two shells left in there," Kelsey called.

"That's all I'm gonna need," Raider replied. "Augie, go!"

Two gourds flew in front of the big man. He waited for an instant and then raised the barrel of the Colt. He fired twice, a pair of quick bursts. To Augie's amazement, both clay gourds shattered into a thousand tiny pieces.

Raider smiled and handed the weapon back to Kelsey. "Doggone good iron, Jake. You got to tell me the name of your gunsmith."

Kelsey holstered the weapon. "Do my own toolin'," he snapped.

"What I thought," Raider replied. "Fine work. Did you rod-out that bore yourself?"

The old gunfighter turned the palomino away. "Reckon y'all will be wantin' to see Henry Masters. Just come this way and we'll hash it out with him. I ain't sure I'm needin' any protection from a Pinkerton. Not even one who shoots like you."

When Kelsey was out of earshot, Augie stepped down and looked up at Raider. "How come you was able to hit them targets with Mr. Kelsey's gun but not your own?"

Raider opened his hand, revealing a fat cartridge that he had palmed out of the cylinder of Kelsey's weapon. "Special loads," the big man replied. "You ever look close at the bore of Kelsey's pistol? It's twice as big as mine, even though the caliber is the same."

Augie grabbed the cartridge to examine it more closely.

Raider pointed to the special round. "He packs it with bird shot. The shell throws a tight, powerful pattern, just like a shotgun. Kelsey's irons are so accurate, I could break two of the gourds with no trouble. Like shootin' ducks in a barrel full of water."

Augie looked hurt. "Hell, it's like he's cheatin'."

"Not necessarily," Raider replied. "He's a showman. If he misses, the folks feel cheated and they want their money back. Nobody gets cheated if he hits the targets and ever'body has a good time."

"Yeah," the little man said disheartenedly.

Raider shook his head. "Heck fire, Augie, I figured you of all people would realize that show folk make their livin' deceivin' the suckers. Am I wrong?"

Augie knew the big man was all too right. "I got work to do," the little man said. "If you need anything, just find me. I'll take care of your mount."

"Will do," Raider replied. "And thanks."

Augie started forward with an energetic spring in his small steps.

Raider pulled his Stetson down over his eyes. He hadn't felt good about showing up Jake Kelsey. He just wanted the old shootist to know that he was a for-real detective, somebody who spotted the tiniest detail. Still, bogus bullets or not, he figured Cougar Jake Kelsey didn't need much protection, especially with those two Colts on his hips.

Raider stiffened a little. It was time to go meet Henry Masters, the head man. And Allan Pinkerton's friend. Best to make a good impression. He could never know when bad news would reach back to the ears of his boss, all the way to Chicago.

Raider wound his way through the crowd of performers and roustabouts, heading for the tall box wagon where Kelsey had tied his palomino. On the side of the wagon, painters were changing HENRY MASTERS' THREE-RING CIRCUS to HENRY MASTERS PRESENTS THE SIX-GUN CIRCUS, WITH COUGAR JAKE

KELSEY, WORLD'S OLDEST LIVING GUNFIGHTER. They were also painting in the face of a lovely young brunette woman. Under her face were the words SEE THE GEORGIA NIGHTINGALE, SONGBIRD OF THE SOUTH.

What was it Pinkerton had said about an older gentleman losing his head over a pretty young face?

As he ascended the steps of the wagon, a voice cried out from behind him. "Beware, cowboy. Beware the Queen."

Raider turned to catch a glimpse of Professor Excalibur's furling cape. The professor fled between the tents and wagons, the black cape flapping in the breeze. A spook, Raider thought. Sometimes people like the crazy old fortune-teller could be useful. And sometimes they could cause a lot of trouble as well.

Best to get on with it. He knocked on the door at the rear of the box wagon. No one told him to enter. When he pressed his ear to the door, he could hear two men arguing. The voice of Jake Kelsey rose above that of the other man. Their words were easily discernible.

"I don't want that Pinkerton around *my* show!"

"Our show, Jake."

Raider rapped harder during a lull in the argument.

"Come in," someone shouted.

Raider entered a smoky wagon to see a comical man in a black derby perched behind a desk. Kelsey was on his feet, leaning toward the derby man with a hateful glare in his eyes. When Kelsey saw Raider, he wheeled around and sat down in a chair.

The man in the derby offered the big Pinkerton a straight-backed wooden chair. He gestured with his cigar. "I'm takin' you to be Raider."

Raider nodded. "You take rightly."

"I'm Henry Masters." The man struck a match, revealing his bulldog face more clearly in the shadowy light of the wagon. He puffed a red tip onto the cigar. "Allan Pinkerton said he was sendin' his best agent to watch over me."

Raider chortled. "Don't know if that's true. Although I did get me a commendation here recent-like."

Masters grunted out a cloud of smoke and coughed. "Guess I'm gettin' old if I have to be nursemaided."

He was older than Raider expected. Over fifty, with a

paunch and plenty of lines on his face. Thin gray hairs stuck out from under the derby. A bottle of whiskey was on his desk.

Looking around, Raider thought that, except for the smoky smell, the interior of the wagon had been done up by a woman. All red curtains and wallpaper. The fancy touch.

Masters pointed to his star performer with the cigar. "Jake here seems to think we don't need you."

Raider shrugged. "Wasn't it his life that was threatened?"

Masters nodded. "Found him sprawled out with a lump on his head. I thought he was dead. And whoever done it took my gold right out from under his nose."

Kelsey looked down at the floor. "I'm not proud of that, Henry." The shootist bit his lip. He looked a lot older close up. The tan didn't quite smooth away all the wrinkles.

Raider still hoped he fared that well when he got old—*if* he ever got that old.

"I admit that I'm slowin' up," Kelsey said. "But I won't be caught off guard again." He slapped his holster. "No siree."

Masters did not seem impressed. "You'd think Jake would welcome a bona fide professional like you. After all, he had to dip into his own pocket after my gold was stolen. That's when he bought in for half."

Raider studied the man in the derby. "Mr. Masters, do you have any idea why someone would want to take your gold?"

"Just because it glitters," Masters replied.

Raider leaned forward a little. "Nobody would want to sabotage your circus? You know, mess it up?"

Masters threw out his hands. "Mister, I been on every end of this business. I've been a clown, a bareback rider, a ringmaster. Why would anyone want to bring down my circus tent? I've never had an enemy in my whole life. That's the long and the short of it."

Masters had a funny way of expressing himself, Raider thought. He was as likable as Kelsey. Why would somebody want to hurt them? Maybe the gold had been the final target of the thief.

Raider hesitated before forcing the next inquiry. "Mr. Masters, don't take this the wrong way, but you were recently married, weren't you?"

Masters nodded. "Yes, but I don't see—"

"Does your wife have any enemies that might want to—"

"Absolutely not," Masters replied vehemently. "And I won't have you besmirching the name of my beloved."

Raider backed off quickly. "I didn't mean nothin' by it. I just have to cover all the edges of the flint rock. I had to ask."

Masters turned to Jake Kelsey. "Jake, do you have any notions as to who might have knocked you out and taken that gold?"

Kelsey seemed to become more cooperative. He leaned forward a little, as if he wanted to speak in a confidential tone. I'm glad you asked me that. If you want my word on it, I think that crazy fortune-teller had somethin' to do with it."

Raider could not contain an involuntary laugh. "Professor Excalibur?"

Masters smiled. "I see you've already met him."

Raider eased back in his chair, shaking his head. "He did seem a mite addlepated, but he don't seem like the kind to harm someone."

Kelsey bristled. "Mark my words, big 'un, he's plumb loco."

Masters looked rather doubtful. "Excalibur's been with me for more than ten years. He's eccentric, but—"

"He's a couple of logs shy a cord," Kelsey insisted. "He's been badmouthin' the circus too. Sayin' we ain't payin' him enough money."

Raider considered it more closely. "Mr. Kelsey might be onto something here. Sometimes insane people can do things you'd never figure they could pull off. I seen it before. One time, when I was with my old partner, we had to hunt down this boy who had somethin' weird growin' inside his head. Stole a whole bunch of silver up to Medicine Bow. He was as wild as a Comanche squaw and then some."

Masters remained adamant. "I can't believe that Excalibur would steal from me after all these years. And if he did take that gold, why would he hang around here?"

"To avoid suspicion," Raider replied. "Then he could leave later on, when nobody was lookin'. Maybe I will talk to him first."

Kelsey shook a crooked finger at Raider. "Mark me, both of you, that loose-brained fortune-teller could very well be the one."

"I'm sure Raider can talk to him," Masters said. "And you should feel free to question anyone else in the troupe."

Raider inquired as to the schedule for bringing up the big show. The first performance was set for a week away, right there in Kansas City. Afterward, the show would head west on a predetermined route. They'd try to hit the bigger towns, but they also planned to play for any place that could muster a couple of hundred willing citizens with coins in their pockets.

"I want to know exactly where we're goin' at all times," Raider said. "If there's a lawman around, I want him to know we're comin' before we get there. I may even ask for somebody to cover our backs if things get tight. You can't be . . . oh." He took off his Stetson and stood up. "Excuse me."

A woman moved in behind Henry Masters. She had sprawling brunette hair, soft white skin, pampered hands, and the face of angel—the same face that was being painted on the wagon. Large, firm breasts underneath a high-necked dress. She bent down and gave Masters a peck on the cheek.

Raider thought she had the looks and face to make any man lose his head. Small waist, big hips. He had to beat out the fire that burned inside him, trying not to dote on her healthy chest.

"My wife," Masters said. "Ramona, I'd like you to meet Raider. He's here to make sure we don't have any more trouble."

When she spoke in her breathy voice, the Southern accent came through thicker than molasses. "I'm sorry to interrupt, gentlemen, but I needed to see Henry."

Kelsey stood up. "I'll show Raider around the camp."

Raider stood up. Ramona Masters smiled at him. Raider wondered if he imagined the twinkle in her eye. They were all silent for an awkward moment. Raider just stood there, twirling his Stetson in his hands, his eyes focused on the floor.

Finally Ramona said, "Do call on us for dinner, Mr. Raider. Henry says I'm almost as good a cook as the fat lady. Although I do have to watch my girlish figure."

Masters patted his middle-aged girth. "Not me, honey. I love to eat everything she cooks."

Kelsey stepped in between Raider and Ramona. "Come on, big man, I'll be showing you around the camp. Let you get to know the whole bunch."

Masters eyed the old shootist. "So you're agreeable to Mr. Raider stayin' on, Jake?"

Kelsey forced a smile. "Can't argue with playin' it safe. I reckon I am a couple of steps slower than I used to be."

Masters grinned. "Couldn't have anything to do with Raider catching on to your special loads?'

Kelsey sighed. "He was quick to pick that up."

Masters looked at the rough-hewn Pinkerton. "I hope you don't tell anybody that Kelsey here is packin' show guns."

Raider shrugged. "I didn't see nothin'. His secret is safe with me."

Masters laughed. "Pinkerton was right, Raider, you are a good man."

"Oh, I don't know about that," he replied. "But I will say that you won't be sorry I stayed, Mr. Masters. If there is somethin' goin' on around here, I'll get to the bottom of it. If there's any way possible, I'll get your gold back for you."

"I'm sure you will." Masters nodded. "I'm sure you will."

He gave his young wife a pat on her ample backside. Raider was embarrassed by the explicit gesture. He quickly took his leave, donning his Stetson as he and Kelsey emerged into the heat of the afternoon. Summer was beginning to overtake the Kansas plain.

Kelsey straightened his own white Stetson to stave off the glare. "I reckon you want to see that fortune-teller first."

Raider hesitated. "Jake, if you don't care, I'd like to look around by my lonesome."

"These folks might not take to a stranger," Kelsey offered.

"Maybe not, but these kind are quick to gossip. I'm pretty sure they all know who I am by now and why I've come here. The word has spread through them like wildfire, if I'm right."

Kelsey frowned. "Suit yourself. I got plenty of work to keep me busy. You can have the run of the place for all I care." He strode off without saying goodbye.

Cougar Jake sure as hell didn't mince words. He hadn't been too keen on Raider hanging around, but then he had turned in the other direction in a hurry. Kelsey was a funny one, although Raider figured he might be nervous about the big show. After all, the *World's Oldest Living Gunfighter* was the center-ring main attraction.

Raider thought about the woman, Ramona Masters, the Georgia Nightingale. Had she gazed a little too fondly at him? Her husband hadn't thought so, the way he had patted her butt right there in front of them. Masters wasn't the kind to appeal to a younger woman. Had Ramona come along for the ride?

Reaching for a bandanna in his back pocket, Raider mopped his brow. He'd go see the old professor first. Excalibur. What kind of name was that? Doc would have known if he was still around.

Suddenly Augie was beside him, tugging at his leg. "Hey? How are you doin', cowboy?"

"Just fine, little . . . er, Augie."

Augie pointed toward the wagon. "What did Mr. Masters have to say?"

"Not much," Raider replied. "Say, tell me somethin', Augie. What the hell kind of a name is Excalibur anyway?"

The little man laughed and started to tell him.

CHAPTER EIGHT

"Excalibur was King Arthur's sword," Augie said. "King Arthur was with the knights of the Round Table. He had a magician, Merlin, who did all kinds of magic to make sure Arthur stayed on as king."

Raider nodded. "Seems like a fittin' name for a man who makes his livin' by doin' magic." He looked down at Augie. "Was this Excalibur a magic sword?"

"Far as I know."

Raider put the bandanna back in his pocket. "Well, Augie, you could help me out if you'd just tell me where this carzy Excalibur hangs his hat. Think you could do that for me?"

"That I can do! Easy." He was awed to be helping the Pinkerton. "Come along. I always know where to find Excalibur. He's—"

A hollow rattling scared the little man. A wooden bucket had been tossed at Augie, crashing into the steps of a nearby wagon. Striding out of the sun came a broad-shouldered man, bare to the waist, holding an iron sledge. He was shorter than Raider, but about fifty pounds heavier.

"Augie! The shit's ass-deep in the camel's cage. Get over there and shovel it out!"

He had hateful, white-ringed eyes and a low tilt to his brow.

Raider stiffened a little. "Augie's helpin' me, pardner."

The man rested the sledge on his shoulder. "And who might you be?"

"Pinkerton agent," Raider said, hoping to avoid a confrontation with the big roustabout. "I'm investigating the theft of some gold. Would you happen to know anything about it, Mr. . . ."

The man wheeled away from him, heading into a crowd of stagehands.

"Not a friendly one," Raider said.

Augie glared at the big man. "I'm certainly glad you didn't come to fisticuffs with that brute. Although a strange gleam was in your eyes."

Raider looked doubtful. "What gleam?"

"Like you thought you could kick his ass."

Raider scoffed. "I was just takin' offense to the way that ape was barkin' at a little . . . I mean, at you, Augie."

Augie waved him off. "That's just Bull. Bull Harmon. He's the chief of the tent crew."

Raider nodded slowly. "Still, he didn't seem to want you to be around me. Could that mean anything important?"

"I do have to clean the camel's cage," Augie said.

"I'll talk to him sooner or later. Hey, Augie, what the devil is a camel?"

Augie laughed. "Don't worry, you'll know it when you see it." He picked up the bucket and then pointed straight ahead. "Just follow the line of wagons till the end. The professor's is usually the last one. Don't worry, you'll know which wagon is his."

With that, the dwarf waddled off toward the cage of the mysterious camel creature. Raider walked with him a ways. Augie was turning out to be good company.

They strode along the row of wagons. Raider saw some of the performers in more compromising positions, particularly some of the females, who seemed to think that lounging around in their underwear was the proper thing to do. He had to pull himself away from the wagon of the snake lady. In spite of his aversion to reptiles, Raider demonstrated a fervent regard for the woman beneath the serpent.

"Will you come on," Augie said disgustedly. "Snakes. Ugh."

Raider tipped his hat and fell in beside his helper. "If I can just get her out of that monster. What the hell kind of snake is that, anyway?"

"A python," Augie replied. "There, I believe that hovel belongs to the man you want. I'll see you later." The little man hurried off to his task.

Was there any doubt that he had located the dwelling of a madman? Raider wondered. He had seen some spooky things in his time as a detective, but he had never seen anyone work so hard as Professor Excalibur. The old man had raised a flour-sack tent over an ancient buckboard. His tent was large enough to create a sizable enclosure. The professor sat cross-legged on the buckboard, surrounded by heaped-up boxes of his magic.

"Auuuommm," he chanted as Raider pulled back the drape that served as his front door.

Raider affected his best Southern manners as he asked, "Mind if I come in, Professor?"

"Abandon hope all ye who enter here," the professor moaned. He held up a Tarot card. "For you are dead! Dead for a ducat!"

The professor struck a sulphur match and torched the end of the card, which bore the image of the Grim Reaper.

Raider shook his head. "Sounds like mumbo-jumbo to me."

Excalibur cried, "Ha!" and broke a small egg in front of Raider's face. A tiny bird flew out of the egg and winged through the hot air of midday. It was an easy trick. Raider thought he had seen it somewhere before.

"The Angel of Death," Excalibur bellowed. "Flying to those who would harm Henry Masters."

Raider stepped into the musty flour-sack balloon and stood in front of the old trickster. Excalibur proceeded to perform a series of sleight-of-hand tricks that were impressive but by no means original—shuffling cards, making the aces dance out of the deck, fluttering the kings and queens.

Raider wondered if he was going to get any straight answers from the magician. Excalibur seemed to have taken leave of his senses. There was nothing to do but try.

"Professor," Raider started, "are you knowin' anythin' about that gold what was stole?"

Excalibur ignored him, staying with his card tricks.

"Come on, boy," Raider urged. "It looks a lot better if you talk to me. People might say you's hidin' somethin' if you keep quiet."

Still no response.

"Shit," Raider groaned. "You know, I'd really like to see some method to your madness, old man, but I . . ."

Suddenly the professor looked up at him, his eyes almost in tears. He unfolded his legs and slid down off the buckboard. Raider wondered if the old boy was about to lose it, but instead Excalibur reached out to shake Raider's hand.

"Shakespeare," Excalibur said softly. "What do you know of Shakespeare?"

Raider shrugged. "Come again?"

"A method to my madness. *Hamlet*. You recited from *Hamlet!*"

"Er, sure," Raider replied.

Actually he was only reciting something he had heard his former partner say a hundred times. But if it would draw out Excalibur, he would play along. Better to humor someone who was riding with a loose saddle.

"To be or not to be," Excalibur replied, "that is the question."

"Well," Raider offered, "you seem to know about that stuff."

Excalibur raised an eyebrow. "Know? Nay it is, I know not know! I was Shakespeare, the embodiment of the Bard himself. My name was Raleigh Edwards. When I was much younger, before the ravages of drink and old age, I performed all of the Bard's folio." He strutted back and forth, gesticulating grandly. "I was Macbeth, Lear, Prospero."

"And I'm sure you were a good 'un, to," Raider said, flattering the man.

Excalibur drew his cape around him. "As good as Booth or Kean. And now . . ." His voice sank and his body seemed to deflate. "Now, I am reduced to the mockery of tricks and cards."

"You ain't half bad, though."

Excalibur wheeled around and resumed his sitting position on the back of the buckboard.

He was completely out of his mind, but harmless. Raider was almost sure of that. The old man stiffened proudly. "You wished to speak to me, sirrah?"

Raider nodded. "I'd like to ask you a few questions."

"Lay on, Macduff!"

"Raider's the name." He hesitated before asking, "What do you know about Jake Kelsey and the attempt on his life?"

"Nothing," was the curt reply.

"What about Henry Masters?"

Excalibur did not waver. "Good man. The king. More than kin and less than kind." He flashed the appropriate Tarot card. "He is my Arthur, I am his Merlin. It is Mordred that you seek."

Raider decided not to ask who Mordred was. Instead he asked, "And Ramona Masters?"

Excalibur recoiled, making a hissing sound that had no doubt greeted him toward the end of his days on stage. "Eve did the apple eat and doomed Adam to live outside the Garden of Eden for all eternity."

Raider was growing tired of the riddles. "Mr. Edwards, I need details. I want to find Mr. Masters's gold and the man who hit Jake Kelsey over the head. If you don't—"

Excalibur flashed a card in front of his eyes. "Ask the knave. He will lead you to the evil."

"Kelsey thinks you stole his gold," Raider blurted out.

Excalibur began to laugh hysterically. "The knave!"

Raider would have pressed him for real names if something extraordinary had not transpired. As if by Excalibur's crazy conjuring, a young woman appeared under the far edge of the tent. Her face came through first, smooth and frightened. The rest of her petite body squirmed into the tent. She bolted upright and started to brush the sawdust from her maroon leotard.

Raider gawked at her beautiful form until the woman spoke in a sweet Spanish voice. "Señor, are you not the detective who has come to help Señor Masters?"

"I reckon I am, but—"

She held up her hand. "Shh. I must be quick, for he is

following me. I must speak to you tonight, after dark, when we have finished our rehearsal."

Raider felt himself being drawn to the woman's aristocratic manner. She held herself with the posture of a queen, in spite of her distress. Her steps were like that of a ballerina as she glided to the tent opening to peer out onto the circus grounds. What was she afraid of?

"You got a name?" Raider inquired.

She peered back at him with huge brown eyes. "I am Ilana. I ride the bareback horse. You will see. I will explain later."

Raider could not help but notice her tightly muscled body beneath the leotard. "Maybe we ought to talk now."

"No!" She snapped it out. "I must leave before I am seen. He will not leave me in peace."

"There you are!" The voice resounded above the noise of the encampment.

Raider looked out to see the man known as Bull Harmon walking toward the professor's slapdash tent. Ilana trembled at the sight of the hulking foreman. He gestured with his thumb, pointing back toward the corral.

"They's wantin' you over to the ring, lady," Harmon shouted. "Best be gettin' back." When she hesitated, he added, "Now, woman!"

As she started to move, Raider gently put his hand on her shoulder. "Sit still, honey. You're talkin' to me." He turned back toward Bull to see if he had any objections.

Harmon glared at Raider. "You tryin' to tell me how to run my business, rube?"

Raider smiled. "Name's Raider, Pinkerton National Detective Agency. And the last time I checked, this business belonged to Henry Masters. He's done give me the run of the place."

Harmon squinted at the challenge, his fists tight. He knew the fight was going to happen, the same way Raider knew it. The questions were only *when* and *where*. *If* had already been decided.

Ilana pushed Raider's hand away. "Please, I must go." She cast a quick look toward his black eyes. "Tonight." Then she was gone, rushing past the massive roustabout who still glared at Raider.

"You're gettin' a good look, Harmon," the big Pinkerton challenged again.

Excalibur moved forward. "Sir, I don't think it wise that you—"

Raider put a hand in the professor's chest. "Back off, Excalibur. This is between me and the hombre here. Ain't that right, Bull?"

Harmon showed bare teeth. "Maybe you're just lookin' to get your back broke, cowboy."

Excalibur was trembling. "Mr. Raider," he said hoarsely, "I daresay this is the last thing you need right now."

Raider took off his Stetson. "No, Professor, this is just what I need. Seems like there's two kinda folks hereabouts, them that want to help and them that don't. Bull there is the biggest, meanest obstacle that they got to offer. If I stand up to him in their territory, it might just make things a little easier down the road."

Excalibur thought that Raider made sense in a strange, savage way. He eyed the stout frame of the heavier roustabout as if he had been wanting someone to shut Harmon's mouth. "Do you really think you can best him?"

Raider laughed and started to unbuckle his gunbelt. "I reckon we'll find out now, won't we?"

"He's a savage knave," Excalibur muttered.

Raider handed his holster to the old magician. "Just be waiting with the bandages in case I get the tar kicked out of me."

Harmon was turning away as Raider strode out of the tent.

"Hey, sheep dip," Raider called.

Harmon stopped dead in his tracks.

Raider kept on. "You want to answer some questions for me, pardner?"

Harmon leered sideways at him. "Go shit in your hat, Pinkerton." He started away, heading toward the corral.

"Didn't think you'd be the kind to run, Harmon." Raider had said it in his worst mocking voice.

Harmon swung around with a half smile on his face, as if he didn't believe that Raider was forcing his hand so early. "You want to fight, Pinkerton?"

Raider shrugged. "Not if you're gonna turn tail and run. I

can't hit a man in his backside. Not if he's playin' chicken."

A jolt rippled through Harmon's muscles. "Don't tempt me, Pinkerton. Don't tempt me to take your head off."

Raider smiled. "Answer my questions and we can avoid the rough stuff."

"No questions, no answers," Harmon replied.

"Then we fight," Raider said. "Time and place, gopher face!"

Harmon pointed a balled-up fist at Raider. "Now! Main corral. Give me five minutes to drum a crowd and take bets."

"You're on, fat boy!"

Harmon stormed away with a ferocity that had no doubt earned him the appropriate first name.

Raider's brave smile eased back into a look of uncertainty. "Well, I do believe that fat-boy part got him."

Excalibur moved next to him. "You don't seem as sure of yourself."

Raider was counting on one thing. Big men like Harmon didn't have to fight much because most people were afraid of them. But what if he could fight? Raider entreated the professor to bury him deep so the coyotes couldn't get at his carcass. Excalibur cackled with laughter.

Raider just shook his head. "Let's go."

"Lay on, Macduff, and damned be he who first cries, 'Hold, enough.'"

With Excalibur beside him, Raider started for the corral.

A good fight doesn't just happen, it builds. The crowd begins to grow, money changes hands, the contestants stand across from one another trying to look intimidating. Each man faces the challenge of besting another man who's wanting to bash his brains out.

Onlookers clung to the corral railing like insects swarming to a fresh carcass. Raider sort of enjoyed them, even though he knew they would be rooting for Bull Harmon. They'd always root for their own, despite the fact that Harmon was by no means popular.

Bull flexed his arms, sweat glistening on his shoulders.

Raider kept his shirt on to protect him from the heat. He had also taken a couple of dippers full of water. He wondered how the heat would affect his stamina.

Excaliber stepped next to Raider and handed him a small vial of powder. "Swallow this."

Raider shook his head. "I don't think—"

"Do it," the old man whispered, "or you'll drop in the first five minutes from the heat."

Raider reluctantly palmed the vial, lifting it to his lips. The powder was dry and salty. The big man felt a tug at his pants leg. He looked down to see Augie offering him another dipper of water. Raider washed down the powder with a short swallow.

Augie took back the dipper. He was staring at Bull Harmon. "It's about time he picked on somebody his own size." His expressive eyes rolled up at Raider. "Better watch the Bull. He cheats."

Raider exhaled. "Yeah, I reckon he would."

Harmon had picked up his sledge to swing it over his head like a toy hammer. He was strong. Raider stepped forward and drew the line in the dirt. Harmon froze, his eyes narrow, the sledge in front of him.

Raider pointed to the hammer. "You think you're gonna need that to best me, boy?"

Harmon flung the hammer to the ground. "All I need are these." He held up his hands.

The audience tittered as Harmon lumbered toward the mark Raider had drawn with his boot. Raider's toe rested on the center point of the line.

Harmon dropped his boot on the mark.

Raider swung immediately, catching him near the temple but in the hard part of his skull. Harmon grunted and took a step backward. Raider's hand stung. He quickly moved sideways as Harmon laughed and came after him.

Bull was slow. Raider used some fancy footwork to stay away from the powerful rights and lefts that Harmon brought up from the basement. Every time Harmon missed, his face became redder and he redoubled his efforts.

When the feeling came back into his right hand, Raider started to lay it in on Harmon's face, peppering him with short, waspish blows. Blood ran from Bull's nose, trickling down his chest. He stopped to touch the crimson line on his mouth.

Someone from the audience yelled, "Get him, Bull!" and suddenly the crowd was behind their bleeding gladiator.

A guttural cry welled up out of Harmon. He charged Raider, driving him into the railing of the corral. Raider grunted as his breath left his lungs. Harmon's knee in his gut didn't help matters any.

Raider wanted to vomit, and then he wanted to die. His head seemed disconnected from the rest of his body. He willed his arms to fight back, but they did not respond.

Harmon pulled him up by the shirt. "Big man Pinkerton, huh. You don't look so tough now."

All Raider could do was spit. So he did. Right in Harmon's face. Bull yelled maniacally, flinging Raider toward the center of the corral. Raider stumbled for a few steps before he hit and rolled. When his eyes turned up to the hot sky, he felt water in his face. He opened his mouth for a swallow of the cold, bitter liquid. What was that taste? Had Excalibur slipped another potion into the dipper?

Raider's eyes focused on Augie, who hovered over him. "You still rootin' for me, Augie?"

"Get up. He's coming after you!"

Augie tried to help him up. But Harmon beat him to it. He pulled Raider off the ground and started slapping him like a scarecrow. It didn't hurt, really. In fact, Raider thought it was waking him up. Or was it that water with the professor's strange powder?

Raider's left hand straightened out in Harmon's face, snapping his head back. The right lifted in a crushing uppercut to Bull's chin. Suddenly the roustabout's eyes were glassy.

Raider shook his head. His senses had returned. He began to stalk Harmon with skills honed over years of fighting. Harmon tried to back away lifting his arms to fend off the punches.

Augie cried, "Beat him, Raider!"

Suddenly a whole faction of the audience was rooting for the big Pinkerton. Bull had picked on a lot of people. Raider heard cries from the bareback rider and the snake woman. They were on his side.

With Harmon's guard up over his face, Raider dropped down to slam a couple of fists in his gut. Harmon grunted and doubled over. Raider brought up a knee that caught Bull in the forehead, knocking him to the ground. Harmon wallowed on his back, moaning like a sick mule.

"More!" Augie cried. "Give it to him!"

Raider shook his head. "He's had enough. Haven't you, Bull?"

Harmon did not reply.

Raider turned away to meet eyes with the snake lady. She still had that python draped around her neck, wound in her red hair, covering her large breasts. If he could just get that snake away from her long enough to . . . he saw a sudden spark of panic in the snake lady's green eyes. She grimaced and pointed over Raider's shoulder.

The big man turned in time to see Bull Harmon rushing him out of the sun. Harmon had the sledge raised above his head. Raider ducked him but the sledge grazed his leg. Harmon swung around again, crashing the hammer into the railing. Splinters flew from the timber.

Raider limped away from the madman, rubbing his shin.

Harmon kept coming, swinging the steel sledge with all his might, barely missing Raider with each determined thrust.

Finally Raider let him get close. When he reached backward with the sledge, Raider dropped down and swung his legs out in a sweeping move that his former partner had taught him. Harmon tumbled sideways, banging his head on the handle of the sledge.

Raider staggered to his feet. Harmon was right with him. He picked up the hammer and began a slow stalk, backing Raider toward the fence.

"You're dead now, Pinkerton. And I'm the one who's gonna kill you."

With his wolf eyes and the blood on his face, Harmon looked like a demon from hell.

Raider hadn't wanted to do it, but now he had no choice. His hand dropped to his boot. He brought up the hunting knife that he kept hidden for last chances. Harmon froze at the sight of the gleaming blade.

"Little different, ain't it, bull?" Raider turned the knife in his hand. "Now we're both loaded for bear."

"We don't need this," Harmon said suddenly.

"Then drop the hammer. And I drop the knife."

Harmon tossed the sledge away. Raider buried the knife in

the plank of the corral railing. They squared off again, circling like a couple of brown bears.

Harmon rushed Raider, but this time the Pinkerton was ready—he swung a leg in Bull's path, sending him to the ground again. When he rose to his feet, Raider was in his face, pounding him with rights and lefts for which Harmon had no defense.

Bull teetered like a drunken man. Raider had to admit the boy was tough—slow and stupid, but tough. Finally, Raider didn't feel like hitting him anymore. He turned to walk away.

"Where you goin'?" Harmon cried.

"He beat you, Bull," someone said from the crowd.

"Yeah," came another voice. "Give it up, Harmon."

"No! Never! He didn't beat me!"

Harmon grabbed the knife from the fence. The snake lady cried out as he drew back to hurl it at Raider. Everyone gasped as the blade flew through the air. Raider managed to drop out of the way at the last second. But Harmon was right there with the hammer again.

Raider saw the huge shadow against the sun. Harmon had the sledge over his head. When he tried to roll, he felt a cramp in his right side. He couldn't move a muscle.

Harmon bellowed like an elk.

Raider closed his eyes.

A loud explosion absorbed the sounds of the crowd.

Harmon cried out again.

The sledge head had broken away from the hammer, falling on the roustabout's back. Harmon crashed to the ground next to Raider. Cougar Jake Kelsey walked into Raider's field of vision. His six-guns were smoking. The special loads had given him enough firepower to sever the sledge from its handle.

Raider sat up, massaging the cramp in his leg. "Much obliged, Jake. Reckon you saved me a headache. Some fancy shootin', too."

Kelsey dropped the guns in his holsters. He put a pointed toe in Harmon's ribs. "Git up, you ape."

Augie leaned over the fallen man. "He might be hurt. That sledge may have broken his back."

Kelsey kicked him again. "Ain't nothin' wrong with him. Git up, I say. Git up before I shoot you."

Harmon moaned and scrambled to his feet. He staggered off as if he were blind drunk. Raider also got up, waiting for the cramp to diminish before he started walking again.

Kelsey regarded him. "You okay, pilgrim?"

Raider nodded.

"Had him whupped fair and square," Kelsey said. "He's one to hit those smaller than him. Thinks he has a way with the ladies, too. 'Bout time he got some of his own medicine."

Henry Masters pushed his way through the crowd, demanding to know what had happened. When Kelsey told him, Masters just shook his head. "Bull will get over it. Every man gets whipped once in his life."

Kelsey scowled at his partner. "I say we ought to get rid of him. He's just gonna cause trouble."

"Can't," Masters replied. "He's the best tent man in the business. I need him."

Raider had to agree with Cougar Jake. "He's right, Mr. Masters. That kind can hurt you down the road."

Masters looked perturbed. "Gentlemen, I won't be having you tell me how to run my circus. Now, I need Bull Harmon to make this show function properly. He stays. Don't worry, he'll take his whipping like a man. I'll speak to him personally."

With that, the petulant circus promoter stormed back to his wagon, no doubt to have lunch with his beautiful young wife.

Raider felt the tugging on his trousers again.

Augie looked up at him, holding a wad of cash. "I won all of this, betting on you."

"Good for you," Raider replied.

Cougar Jake paid no mind to the little man. "I have to practice my shooting, gentlemen." He watched Masters for a moment and then headed to the other end of the corral.

Raider rubbed his chin. "Is it my imagination, or is there an awful lot of bad blood between them fellers?"

"Which ones?" Augie offered. "Mr. Kelsey or Mr. Masters? Mr. Kelsey or Bull Harmon?"

"Take your pick," Raider replied. "I don't want to make more of it than there is. I mean, there can be a whole lot of ruckus in raisin' a production like the Six-gun Circus. Still . . ."

He looked at Augie. "Why doesn't Kelsey like Bull Harmon?"

Augie shrugged. "Ain't for me to say." He rolled his eyes back up at Raider. "Are you going to live?"

The big man nodded. "I think so. Nothin' broken. I'm all in one piece, even if the piece is black and blue."

"Someone else is thankful for that," Augie said, nodding toward the adoring snake lady who lingered by the fence.

Raider waved at her, but said to Augie, "Later. Right now I the voluptuous snake lady. She puckered her lips and then Tie some strings together."

Augie beamed. "I know just the place."

He started off, leading the way.

Raider glanced back over his shoulder for one more look at the voluptuous snake lady. She puckered her lips and then smiled at him. He shivered, wondering if she slept with that damned python.

Maybe he'd get a chance later on to find out for himself.

Until then, he had a hell of a lot of thinking to do.

CHAPTER NINE

For such a little man, Augie sure was a big help. He had invited Raider into his tent, which had been set up with all the comforts of home. Augie even had a bottle of whiskey that he had offered to the big man to help him in his cogitations. Now that he was working alone, Raider had to do twice as much thinking, something that he was gradually growing used to.

Sometimes he cussed Doc for leaving the service to marry that pretty woman. But other times Raider wondered if he might not be wise to do the same thing himself. Raider downed a half glass of red-eye, turning his mind back to the task at hand. He stood up and stretched, working out the aches and pains in his body. A fight always left him sore, especially a knock-down-drag-out like the brawl with Bull Harmon.

Raider looked at Augie, who was stirring a huge pot of stew that bubbled over an open fire. "Smells good."

Augie just grunted and kept up his stirring.

Raider went back to the whiskey bottle. He could hear Allan Pinkerton's protests as he poured himself a cupful. Liquor was the damnedest stuff, Raider thought, you could drink a small amount of it and it seemed to clear your head, while too much could do exactly the opposite.

He raised the cup to his lips, wondering when he could

start laying out what he had learned. Sometimes it just had to ferment in his head until the picture was clear. He decided to go outside, where the air was fresh.

"Don't go too far," Augie called. "This stuff'll be ready soon."

Raider nodded. He adjusted his saddle on the ground, stretching out his long legs. Augie had stabled his mount earlier, leaving him the saddle and the horse blanket for a bed. Raider's eyes sagged until he was off into sleep, dreaming of bizarre things until a tin plate rattled him back to the real world.

Augie handed him a plate full of stew and a hunk of bread. "You nodded off there, Raider."

The Pinkerton sat up, wiping his eyes. "I had this crazy dream with women and snakes runnin' all over the place."

"Spare me," Augie replied. "I hate snakes."

Raider leaned back against the saddle, dipping a spoon into the gravy from the stew. "How do you feel about women?"

Augie shrugged. "I like the little ones. Had me a gal once, a dwarf just like me."

"What happened?"

"Ran off to another circus that offered her more money," the little man replied sadly. "Wasn't meant to be."

Raider nodded. "Well, as far as I can see, there ain't but two things that are important to a woman—what she wants and what she wants."

Augie laughed. "How's the stew?"

"Good." Raider sighed and put down the plate. "Reckon I ain't much hungry, though."

Augie frowned. "What's botherin' you?"

"This case," Raider replied. "Ain't got much. Course, it ain't the first time. But as far as I can see, there's this old man who's lost his head for a young thing from Georgia. He's payin' a price. It comes high. Ole Masters there has had to slap together these two shows to try to bring his circus back in the chips. That young cooter is costin' him plenty."

Augie nodded. "But what does that have to do with somebody knockin' Kelsey over the head and takin' all that gold?"

Raider shrugged. "Maybe nothin'. Maybe ever'thing. Maybe old Kelsey has got some enemy he don't know about. He's been around long enough to make more'n a few. Somebody coulda been out for revenge and then just got lucky to find that gold." Raider rubbed his chin. "Course, if somebody did have a notion to get back at Kelsey, they coulda just kilt him right there. Which leads me to another set of deer tracks."

"What might that be?" Augie asked.

Raider tipped back his Stetson. "The most obvious thing is that somebody in the circus company coulda stole the gold and now is layin' low. And I'm figurin' to put Bull Harmon's name high on the list of suspects. He seems to have a grudge agin' Kelsey." He turned his black eyes on the little man. "Augie, do you know of any bad blood twixt Kelsey and Harmon?"

Augie rolled his eyes away. "Some say it's a woman."

"That bareback rider?" Raider asked.

Augie shook his head. "I don't keep up with that kind of gossip. Not close-like anyway."

Raider mulled it over. Women could be a lot of trouble. Still he didn't have much to go on—a few ruffled tempers in the troupe. And show people could just be like that, naturally mean to one another. Besides, he doubted Kelsey cared much for women at his age. It probably took all of the old coot's energy just to keep up with his shooting.

Augie was staring at the big man. "You look like you're a hundred miles away from here."

He sighed. "I'm just considerin' things that might not be easy to see right at first."

"Like what?"

Raider shrugged. "I ain't sure you want to hear it, not the way you seem to like your boss."

"Try me," Augie said warily.

"All right," Raider replied. "Every coin has got two sides, and sometimes you just have to say what could be." He straightened his body. "Let's say that ole Masters there is hurtin' for geetus. Wouldn't it help to knock out Kelsey and take back all that gold? Masters could pretend he was broke and then make Kelsey cough up his life savin's for the rest of the money to keep the show goin'."

Augie gaped at the big man. "How can you say such things?"

"Ain't no secret what can be hidden in a man's heart,

Augie. I seen people rob their own kin. Greed can do strange things to a man. Or a woman."

Augie pointed his spoon at him. "Leave Ramona out of this. She's as decent a woman as they come."

"Excalibur didn't seem to have such a high opinion of her," Raider replied. "Compared her to Eve eatin' the apple."

"What does he know?" Augie grumbled. "She's a fine lady."

Raider grinned slyly. "You sure you ain't holdin' back on me, Augie? Seems like you're workin' the horse too hard to defend her."

"I'm not doing anything," Augie cried. "Oh, damn you!"

He threw the spoon at Raider, barely missing his head. He started to run away, but Raider caught him and lifted him off the ground like a child in the middle of a tantrum. Augie's legs and arms flailed at the big man.

"Steady there," Raider said.

"Let me go, you big galoot."

Raider held him out at arm's length. "I'll put you down if you promise to stay and help me."

Red-faced, Augie finally agreed. When Raider put him down, he went back into the tent. He was clearly through talking for the night.

Raider figured to let the little man steam for a while. When he cooled off, he would be ready to talk again. After all, Augie loved the circus, and he would want what was best for his boss. And only the truth could serve them best. Even if it meant stepping on a few toes.

Returning to his plate of stew, Raider finished eating. The whiskey bottle was close by. The sun was almost gone, and the fire seemed to call for a drink.

But then the woman started screaming in the encampment, so there was nothing for Raider to do but run straight through the dusk, toward the shrill, horrifying sound.

With his hand full of the Colt .45 Peacemaker, Raider hurdled through the evening shadows of the circus camp. He stopped beside a roaring fire, listening until the woman cried out again. The big man launched himself toward the direction of the cries, wondering how long it would take to find her.

The Pinkerton hurled his legs over the tent ropes tracking

the woman's voice as he got closer. She was not only screaming, but seemed to be pleading with someone to leave her
alone. A man's gruff tone punctuated her protests. Raider
thought he heard a flat hand hitting a soft face.

"That son of a bitch!"

He rounded the corner of a wagon to see Bull Harmon
holding the small woman who performed as a bareback rider.
Raider could not remember her name. Bull raised his hand to
strike her again.

Raider thumbed back the hammer of the Colt and barked
off one round.

Bull Harmon grabbed his hand, the one he had raised to hit
the girl.

Raider had amputated the tip of Bull's index finger. Blood
rushed down the arm of the burly roustabout.

"Looks like I have to straighten you out twice in one day,"
Raider said, moving slowly forward. "Back away from the
girl, Bull, or you'll never get another chance to hit a helpless
female."

Harmon growled at the big man. "You're mighty big with
that gun."

"Just think of it as my sledge-hammer," Raider replied.
"Now git away from that woman."

When Harmon backed off, the girl ran toward Raider. She
threw her arms around his waist burying her face in his chest.
The big man stroked her hair, urging her to stop crying.

Before he could sort out what had happened, other
members of the troupe swarmed around them. Kelsey and
Masters were among those who rushed into the throng. Masters demanded to know what had happened.

Raider gestured at Bull Harmon with the bore of his Colt.
"Your boy here figured he'd practice up for our next fight by
slapping around this little woman."

Masters glared at Harmon. "Is this true?"

Harmon did not reply.

Masters looked at the girl. "Ilana, was he bothering you?"

"I just want him to leave me alone," she replied, sobbing.
"He thinks he owns me. Ever since my father passed away, he
has been trying to get me to come to his wagon. I don't want
him. Do you hear? I hate him."

Masters stroked her hair for a moment and then glared at

Harmon. "You're pushing your luck, Bull. If I didn't need you now, I'd send you packing. Now get back to your chores."

Harmon held up his injured hand. "What about this?"

"You had it comin'," Raider rejoined.

Masters waved them away. "Just get a bandage on it."

"You're lettin' him stay on?" Raider asked.

Masters climbed up onto the nearest wagon seat and looked out over the gathering of his company. "Now listen up, all of you. There ain't gonna be no more malarkey on this show. I'm in charge here, and them who ain't in agreement with that can pack up and leave right now. And that goes for Bull Harmon. One more step out of line and he's gone. Is that understood?"

The troupe nodded among themselves.

Harmon slunk away to mend his wounds.

As Masters climbed down, Kelsey stepped closer to Raider. "I knowed we shoulda let him go. Nothin' but trouble," whispered the aging gunfighter.

"He is gone if he makes one more mistake," Masters replied. He glared at Raider. "I thought you were supposed to keep trouble from happenin'. Hell, there's been more trouble since you came."

Raider shrugged. "Sometimes it works that way. If you want your gold back, we might have to smoke out the weasel who stole it."

Masters eyed the drawn Peacemaker. "Raider, are you just gonna shoot everybody until you get a confession?"

"I did what I had to," he replied. "All in the line of duty."

Kelsey intervened, stepping between the big man and the circus promoter. "I'da done the same, Mr. Masters. Harmon had it comin'. The thought of it, pickin' on a little helpless female."

Raider holstered the Peacemaker. "If you don't want me here, Masters, call Pinkerton and he'll send you another boy."

Masters was taken aback at Raider's candor, but finally said, "No, I want you to stay on. If you recover my gold . . . "

"I will."

Masters pointed a finger at him. "But don't you interfere with my show, Raider. I have to bring up the big tent or my carcass will be fodder for every vulture west of the Mississippi. Do you hear me?"

Raider nodded, prompting Masters to storm back to his

wagon and that pretty young wife. Kelsey followed after him, keeping up his protest about Bull Harmon's presence in camp. Raider thought it might be better if the roustabout stayed on—*if* Harmon was involved in the shenanigans.

The rest of the crowd began to disperse, leaving Raider alone with the young bareback rider. Augie stood next to Ilana, consoling her. Her tears were subsiding a bit. Raider studied her face, which was smooth and white, like a china doll. Tiny nose and lips. He got the feeling she might break if he touched her.

Augie saw that Raider was staring at her. "That Harmon," he said disgustedly. "How come he thinks he can pick on somebody like Ilana?"

Raider shook his head. "Same reason he makes you shovel out the shit in the camel cage. Some big people think it makes 'em feel bigger to hurt them that's smaller."

Ilana peered up at Raider with her wide brown eyes. "Please, I must talk to you."

"All right," he replied. "Augie, let's hightail it to your place."

Ilana took Raider's arm as they walked together. Augie held on to her other hand. She was perfectly proportioned; she was lovely. The kind of woman any man could love. For that very reason, Raider had decided that Ilana was off limits. If she could just help him with the investigation, that would be enough. Anything more was strictly out of the question.

The vision of the snake lady flowed through his thoughts until they were back in Augie's tent and Ilana was telling her story in the yellow glow of the flickering candle.

Raider watched as Ilana Espinoza lifted the glass of whiskey to her trembling lips. She was a delicate thing, despite the rigors of her act. It took a great deal of strength and concentration to turn flips on the bare back of a moving horse. Raider could not help but wonder how such a fragile creature had survived the circus life. He remembered that she had mentioned her dead father. Perhaps she had been born into the big top.

She drained the cup and asked for another, a move that did not lessen her angelic quality. As he poured a second cup,

Ilana loosened the knot of her dark hair, allowing her long tresses to spill onto her pallid shoulders. Raider caught himself wondering what it might be like to kiss her. He fought off the urge, bending to his professional duties. Ilana clearly had something that she wanted to tell him.

"Thank you," she said softly as she took the cup. When she had finished the second shot, she raised her eyes to him. "That brute always upsets me so."

He gently took the cup from her fingers. "Why is he after you, Ilana? It seems with all the women in the troupe that he could have his pick."

Ilana perched on the edge of a cot that Augie had set up earlier. "I don't know why he picks on me. He had a woman, although I never saw her. Then she was gone and my father died. That's when he started in on me. I hate him, Señor Raider. He is an animal."

Raider waited a moment while she composed herself. The whiskey seemed to be working. She lowered her eyes. Raider wanted to be easy on her.

"Take your time," he said. "I'm ready to listen."

She sighed like a child who had been crying for a long time. "My family has been in the circus for several generations, back to my great-grandfather in Barcelona. My mother was a bareback rider, my father a horseman. He taught her the act, and then they taught me. I was born under the main tent while the show was going on. I slept in a trunk until I was three years old."

"That sounds like a tough life," the Pinkerton said sympathetically.

She began to sob again. "We had been so happy. And then my mother passed on. I got over that after a while. Then my father left me. I have been so alone."

Raider's heart was breaking. "Don't you have people somewhere? Back in Spain or here in America?"

She shook her head. "We are like gypsies. Go where the circus takes us. The circus is my family, or at least it was until . . ."

"You're doin' fine," he urged. "Keep talkin'."

"*She* came," Ilana replied with a bitterness that was uncharacteristic of her gentle nature. "The circus was fine until that harpy married Henry. Then she took control. Because of her, half the acts were fired. Henry had to put his foot down to keep the loyal people with him."

Raider leaned back. "You mean Ramona Masters."

Ilana nodded.

"But she seems to be from a good family. She's well-bred, talks good," he offered. "And Henry Masters seems to be the one in charge."

The dainty bareback rider shook her head. "Things are not always as they seem. When we were in New York, after we returned from Europe, we were supposed to play to a large audience. Only the arena was so big that the Georgia Nightingale's voice was too small and no one could hear her. She flew into a rage that night. She did not want the circus to go on. Henry canceled the performance because of her. That was the final straw. He was broke by then. He had just enough money to get us west. We played small towns where the Georgia Nightingale could be heard."

Raider frowned. "Interestin'. I wonder if Masters was really hurtin' for money. What about the five thousand dollars in gold?"

"The money that was stolen?"

Raider nodded.

"I do not know where the money came from."

"He could have been holdin' it back," Raider suggested.

Ilana's lips curled in a smirk. "Perhaps he was keeping it to entertain the Georgia Nightingale."

Raider smiled. "You might be on to somethin', little lady."

"Mr. Raider, may I have some more whiskey?"

He poured another cup and waited for her to drink. "Ilana, where did Masters meet Ramona?"

Ilana shrugged. "I am not sure. She first appeared when we were in Paris. The circus was still intact then."

"An American girl over yonder tryin' to make good," he said. "I wonder if she was singin' then?"

"Ha," came the scoffing reply. "Some say she was singing on the streets. *Puta!*" She spat after she said it. The word meant "whore."

Raider took a long look at the girl, wondering if spite had motivated her vitriolic confession. Perhaps Ilana was jealous of Ramona. Maybe she looked at Masters as a replacement for her father. With Ramona on the scene, Masters would not have as much time to devote to his circus family.

Still, at least part of what she said was true. The circus had fallen on hard times. Masters was certainly eager to get his gold back—a fact that precluded Raider's theory that Henry had staged the whole robbery to bilk Kelsey out of half the front money for the tour.

He decided to go in another direction. "Ilana, what do you know about Jake Kelsey?"

The girl's eyes opened wide. "I can tell you much about him. He met Henry right here in Kansas City. Kelsey was doing trick shots, betting men that he could outshoot them."

"You mean in life-and-death shoot-outs?"

She shook her head. "No, just things like he's doing now. He'd have someone throw plates in the air and then he would shoot them with his pistol. At first he would miss, just to get the betting up. Then he would slip in his special cartridges and hit the plates every time."

"A snowbird huckster," he said. "How much did he take Masters for the first time?"

She looked astonished. "How did you know?"

Raider shrugged. "It seems to follow. After he suckered Masters in, he offered him the chance to hook up with a crazy Wild West circus show. Probably canceled the debt as part of the bargain. But hell, that ain't wrong, it's just business."

Ilana touched the back of her hand to her forehead. "I am so tired. I hate all of the excitement. I wish things could be the way they were, before Ramona came."

Raider patted her shoulder. "Lie down, Ilana. Go on. I won't bother you. I promise."

But she did not have any fears of being bothered. Instead, she grabbed Raider's hand and touched her lips to his palm. When he tried to pull away, she wrapped her arms around his shoulders and kissed him with a womanly expertise. Ilana was full of surprises.

"Promise me," she said. "Tell me that you will make the circus the way it was."

"I'll do my best, little punkin'. I swear I will."

Her body seemed to go slack. Raider picked her up and placed her on the cot. She stretched out her arms to him, but he shook his head.

"Sleep," he said softly. "I'll be right here."

She closed her eyes.

"Raider, I was wonderin' if . . . Oh, sorry."

Augie had stuck his head into the tent. Raider put a finger to his lips. Augie started to leave, but Raider stopped him. He lifted the lantern and directed Augie outside.

"I didn't mean to disturb you," Augie said.

"No mind," Raider replied. "Augie, I need answers. Is it true that Ramona Masters has her husband by the short hairs? Say the truth if you know it."

Augie bit his lip. "I won't say."

"Then it's true. Unless you tell me different."

"I won't tell you different."

Raider nodded and started off toward the main encampment.

"Hey," Augie called, "don't leave me alone."

"Take care of the girl," he called back.

He strode between the wagons, toward the quarters of Henry and Ramona Masters. He intended to knock on the door of their wagon and ask some straight questions. But when he heard the commotion inside, Raider slipped next to the small window and listed intently.

Ramona sounded like anything but the Georgia Nightingale as she screeched in her husband's ear. "I want Raider gone! Do you understand me? That ape is causing trouble. Can't you see it?"

Henry's voice was calmer, much smaller. "Ramona, honey, he said he could get my gold back."

"Our gold!" Ramona railed. "Didn't I deliver that money to you when you needed it?"

"Yes, dear."

"Then fire Raider. Send him back to Texas or wherever he came from. I won't have him snooping around, ruining my show."

"Our show," Henry reminded her. "And I'm still in charge. The Pinkerton stays!"

Raider imagined the hateful scowl on her face as she said, "You're a weak, ugly old man. I don't know why I ever married you. I ought to leave you and never come back. You're spineless."

Masters slammed his fist into something. "I won't have you talking to me like that."

"Go to hell!" she cried.

Raider eased back into the shadows as Ramona stormed out of the wagon. She stumbled down the steps and headed toward the corral, stomping off in a tizzy. Raider considered following her, to try to talk to her, but he finally decided that in her present state, she would not be very cooperative.

Instead, he hurried back to his own tent where he awoke Ilana. He asked the bareback rider to trace the route of the circus from New York to Kansas City. When she had done that, the big man leaned back, thinking.

Ilana cast a puzzled glance at the rough-hewn detective. "What are you looking for?"

Raider's brown was wrinkled. He looked at Ilana and Augie. "I got to ask both of you to try to remember. Was there any news of a robbery along the way to Kansas City? I mean in one of the towns where the circus was playin'?"

Augie thought about it, as did Ilana. They both said it at the same time: "Kentucky."

"Lexington," Ilana continued. "A Wells Fargo office was robbed."

Augie jumped up and down excitedly. "The sheriff came and searched everyone, but they didn't find a thing. The agent was killed too."

Raider nodded. "She supplied the gold. But how did she pull it off?"

"Beg your pardon?" Augie said.

"Nothin'," Raider replied.

But Ilana was already catching on. "Do you think Ramona Masters had anything to do with taking that gold?"

Raider shrugged. "Can't say as yet. Somebody might have. But this can all wait till the morning. Ilana, you can sleep here." Raider reached into his boot and withdrew a .38-caliber derringer. "Take this, Augie. Watch over her until I get back."

Augie frowned. "Where are you goin'?"

Raider called back over his shoulder, "To make a quick trip around the camp. I want to make sure nobody's lurkin' in the shadows."

Augie tried to follow him for a few steps but could not

keep up with Raider's long strides. "Where will you be if I need you?"

"Ain't sure," Raider replied. "Just keep a lookout. I won't be far."

"Snakes!" Augie cried. "You can't fool me. I know where you're goin'. With those snakes!"

Raider could hear the diminished voice echoing after him. Augie was smart. The sight of Ilana's firm body had been too much for the big man. Everything else could wait until morning. Besides, he could ask the snake woman about Ramona and Henry Masters. If he was lucky, she would tell him the truth. And if he was really lucky, she would do even more than that.

CHAPTER TEN

Raider had no difficulty finding the snake lady's tent, even in the dark. Her dwelling was set apart from the other campers, who had made sure there was plenty of distance between them and the monstrous python. Apparently they were just as afraid of the snake as Raider was. Still, he was driven by needs that soon made him less fearful of the serpentine creature.

He walked back and forth in front of the tent opening, peering into the lantern-lit enclosure, trying to catch a glimpse of the buxom, red-haired woman. He wondered if she was lying in bed with that damned snake.

On the fourth pass by the tent, a sultry voice called to Raider, "Are you coming in or not?"

Raider stopped in his tracks and slipped up to the entrance of the canvas hovel, out of which wafted strong gusts of incense. He peered into the dim recesses, searching for the woman's voluptuous form.

"Don't be afraid," she said. "He won't bite you."

Raider took a deep breath and went straight into the tent.

The woman's hand reached for the coal-oil lamp. She turned up the flame to give him a better look. Raider thought he had walked into a harem.

She peered up at him with her vibrant green eyes. "Ever

seen anything like this in your life, cowboy?"

"Once," he replied. "On a slave ship."

"I thought slavery was illegal," she teased.

Raider nodded. "It is. That's why I had to kill the fellow who was doin' it."

She reclined on a pile of satin pillows. Overhead were strung long bolts of silk cloth, all of different colors. Brass pots smoldered with the exotic fragrances. Her own body was covered in a sequined leotard that she probably used in her act.

She patted the pillows next to her. "Come sit beside me, Raider."

The big man looked all around. "Where's your critter?"

"Lucifer?" She laughed. "He's all locked up for the night."

Raider eyed her dubiously. "S'pose you prove that to me."

At first she looked sort of pouty, but her sensual lips gradually eased into a smile. "So you want to see him. And I thought you were afraid."

His hand slid down to his holster. "Maybe I am. A little."

She got up off the pillows and moved with graceful steps to the other side of the tent. With a quick hand she removed a piece of silk from a cage that had been constructed from wood and fine-mesh wire. The reddish-brown serpent was curled up inside the cage. It opened its eyes and lifted its head slightly.

"That's some danged critter," Raider said, his eyes transfixed on the python's head. "Biggest damn snake I ever seen."

"Now we've wakened him." She moved back toward Raider and kissed him full on the mouth. When she broke away, Raider found himself suddenly looking at the python again. The woman opened another box and pulled out a rabbit by the ears.

Raider drew back a little. "What are you gonna do with that?"

Her face was suddenly serious. "Lucifer thinks it's feeding time," she replied. "And I'm not going to disappoint him."

She lifted up the mesh cover and dropped the hare into the cage with the python. Raider watched with a morbid curiosity as the snake began to move slowly toward the rabbit. It did not seem to be in any hurry to eat. Gradually the python uncoiled, straightening out half of its body.

The hare was frozen with terror, its brownish eyes meeting

the slits of the yellow-eyed snake. When the python stopped dead still, Raider knew it was over. The strike came quickly, but the snake did not gobble down the hare. Instead, it coiled around the twitching body, tightening until the last breath of life was gone from the smaller creature. After a few moments of uncoiling, the mouth opened and the reptile began to swallow the carcass whole.

Raider shook his head and turned away.

The snake woman grabbed him, wrapping her body around his, her lips seeking his mouth again. Raider kissed her for a long time, but he kept thinking of the python behind them. He broke away finally.

"Don't you want me?" she asked, running her hands down to his crotch. "I want you. I want you inside me. I want you to fuck me until I can't move. Only a man like you can... What's the matter?"

Raider gestured back toward the cage. "Ole Lucifer there has got me spooked."

"Oh, he won't eat you alive. But maybe I will."

She stepped away, reclining on the pillows again. Her fingers loosened the leotard, freeing her breasts. When her legs spread, Raider caught a look at the reddish-orange bush. He had to admit that she was appealing. But the damned snake was watching.

She lifted her hand. "Come on, honey. Drop down between my legs. I want you inside. Hurry, while I'm wet."

Raider shook his head. "I can't. Not in this place. Maybe we could go somewhere else."

The snake woman groaned. "I thought you were a man."

He sighed. "All right. I reckon I'll be going."

"No! Wait!"

She got up and hugged him again, this time pressing her firm nipples into his chest. Raider still couldn't feel right about it. He insisted that they find another place to do it.

The woman reached for her robe. "All right. There are some empty stables over by the corral. We can climb up in the loft. I'll take a blanket in case you're afraid of barn mice."

"Aw, that ain't fair," Raider replied. "Hell, you got a damned dragon sittin' over there. Come on. Hey, what's your name, anyway?"

A wicked smile parted her lips. "Eve, honey. That's what

they call me. Eve and her snake. My real name is Sally."

"I reckon you won't mind if I call you by your real name."

Her hand rubbed his crotch again. "Call me anything you like. Just let me have that thing where I need it."

They practically ran from the tent, heading for the stables. Eve brought along the lantern for light. It took them a few minutes to find the right loft, a wooden floor with hay over it. Eve spread out the blanket and reclined, opening her robe to reveal her naked body.

Raider dropped his pants. The night air had revived him. He felt the growing length between his legs. The musky smell of the snake woman reached his nose. He forgot all about the python.

She spread her legs invitingly. "Get down here, cowboy. I been waitin' for a real man to wander through this carny."

"Seems like you'd have your pick," Raider replied. "You are a good-lookin' lady. A fine woman."

"Men think I want to marry 'em after we do it," she said. "I even tried the big boys, ole Kelsey and that boy you whipped on. Hell, they ain't got what it takes. Either that or they're both interested in another woman."

Raider pulled off his shirt. "Who might she be?"

"How the hell should I know? Are you gonna fuck me or not?"

"Yeah," he replied, "I'm gonna fuck you good."

He took off everything, including his boots. She was breathing hard by the time he lay down next to her. She went sort of wild, grabbing his hard cock, stroking it toward her lips. Her mouth was as adept as any he had known. He figured she had been around in her day.

As she sucked him, she whirled her ass around, dropping her crotch into Raider's face. At first he was put off by the strong scent, but as she worked her hips, his tongue came out to lick her. When he found the right spot, she took her mouth off him and cried out.

"Oh God, cowboy, where'd you learn to do that? Don't stop . . . oh . . . keep it up."

She went down on him again, but she couldn't seem to concentrate.

When her cries reached their peak, Raider rolled her over on her back. She could not be still with his prick dangling near her. She pulled at him, trying to get him into the saddle. When he was on top, she grabbed his cock and guided it to the opening of her crotch. With a quick upward thrust, she impaled herself on him.

"That's it," she moaned. "Yeah, hard. As hard as you can."

Raider obliged her, bouncing her off the hay with each plunging motion of his hips. She grabbed his ass, hanging on for the ride, grunting and whispering obscene things in his ear. No matter how hard he delivered, she wanted more.

"Deep, cowboy. Give it to me deep."

Raider felt his burst rising. He quickened his motion toward the moment of release. Eve barked loudly as he came. She wrapped her legs around his waist to keep him buried inside.

"That was the best I ever had it, cowboy. The best."

Raider tried to roll off, but she wouldn't let him. Instead, she held on, feeling his length as it softened inside her. He lowered his mouth to her nipples, kissing the tight buds, tickling her with his mustache.

When he was completely soft, she let him come out.

Raider leaned back on the blanket that covered the hay. "That was pretty fair for me too, Sally."

Her fingers played in the hair on his chest. "I'm sorry what I said before, about you not bein' a real man."

Raider shrugged. "I just couldn't do it with that snake watchin'. It'd be like doin' it in front of your kin."

She rested her cheek against his chest. "I guess it would be at that. Lucifer is just about the only thing I got. Hell, the way that little bitch is pushing Henry around, I won't even have the circus before long."

Raider thought he saw an opening. "You sure you ain't jealous?"

"Of the Georgia Nightingale? Ha. I wouldn't care if Henry put his dick in a goat if it made him happy. I been with him for five years now, and he's always treated me good."

"How the hell did you get in this line of work anyway?"

She sighed. "My mother. She was Yolanda, the snake woman. I tried to get away from the carny life for a while, but it gets in your blood. After a while you see things different from other people. Damn, so many good citizens have their heads in their asses."

Raider nodded. "I hear you."

She reached down for his flaccid cock, rolling it around in her hands. When it didn't spring back to life, she started talking again. "No, things were better before Ramona came along. Now we don't have nearly as many acts as we used to. She made Henry fire them because she said it took away from her singing."

"Can she sing good?" Raider asked.

Eve snorted. "Ah, she ain't bad. I heard better. We used to have these acrobats and one of the women could sing a lot better."

Raider exhaled. "A man can sure lose his mind over a woman."

Her hand went back to his prick, this time with better results.

"Ha," she exclaimed. "I knew if I played with you long enough you'd come back from the dead."

Raider grew erect. He started to get on top again, but she stopped him. She got up on her knees and straddled his crotch.

"I'm going to ride the horsey," she said.

"More like the saddle horn," Raider quipped.

She slipped him into position and then sat down in one motion.

Raider had to admit to himself that she knew what she was doing. She worked her ass in a hundred different directions, pulling him in and out. She'd go slow and then fast, depending on what felt good to her. It felt damned good to Raider as well.

She collapsed on top of him, brushing her breasts against his face. "You finished yet, honey?"

"No," Raider replied. "Maybe it's time I showed you a trick or two."

He felt her body quiver as she said, "Don't be shy. Give it to me any way you like. Hell, I been married four times, so I reckon there ain't much you can do to surprise me."

Raider put her on her back, throwing her legs over his shoulders. She cried out again as he pumped her for the better part of a half hour. He still didn't reach his second climax.

Her hands rubbed the muscles of his chest. "Oh, honey,

ain't you drained that thing yet?"

"No."

"How do you want me, Raider? Tell me the way."

"Like two dogs."

She cried out, scurrying into position. Raider entered her from behind, grabbing her ass. He worked his hips, pulled her backward onto his shaft.

"This is the way," she moaned. "The best way."

Raider came hard the second time. Eve shook violently, her senses out of control. For a minute the big man thought she was having some sort of fit. But when he started to pull out she begged him not to.

"Just leave it a second longer."

He obliged until his legs began to ache. Then he withdrew and wrapped his arms around her.

Eve kissed his face and neck, moaning with pleasure. "How'd you like to be my fifth husband?" she cooed in his ear.

Raider laughed. "You sell the snake and we'll talk about it."

"Never!" she teased.

They were quiet for a while, except for their breathing. As they started to drift off to sleep, Eve said, "When we wake up, I want you to fuck me again. Will you?"

"If I'm able," Raider replied.

He closed his eyes, wondering why all women couldn't be like Eve, the snake woman. She didn't have any airs, and she didn't seem to require all of the finery. Even whores liked a fancy parlor and nice wallpaper. Eve would probably be like that if they tied the knot, he figured.

Raider was almost gone when he heard the commotion below. At first he thought some animal had wandered in off the plain. Then he heard the woman's voice, followed by a man's. He reached for the lantern and extinguished the flame.

He listened for a while, trying to recognize the voices. The woman was much louder. It was obvious after a few minutes that they were fighting. The man seemed to be pleading with her.

"How much longer can this go on?" he said.

"You have to be patient," she replied.

The man said something that Raider could not make out. He nudged Eve to wake her up. When she roused, he put his finger on her lips.

"Listen," he whispered. "There's somebody below us. See if you can tell who it is."

The woman downstairs blurted out, "Damn it all, I'm tired of your demands."

"But I love you. I want you."

Eve put her mouth close to Raider's ear. "The woman is Ramona Masters. I can't tell about the man. He's talkin' too quiet."

Raider whispered back, "You reckon it's Henry?"

The man below spoke again.

"It ain't Henry," Eve whispered.

Raider wanted to get a quick look, but he couldn't risk moving around, as they might hear him.

"I love you, Ramona. Kiss me. Make love to me. It was good before."

Raider's ears perked. "Is that Bull Harmon?"

Eve shrugged. "Maybe."

There was the slightest sound of a struggle and then the crisp report of a hand slapping a face.

"Is that all you can think about?" Ramona Masters cried. "That Pinkerton is crawling all over the place. He's going to make trouble if we don't do something about it."

"What? What can we do?"

There was a deathly silence before Ramona said, "Leave him to me. I'll take care of him, one way or another."

"One kiss, Ramona."

Another silence while she gave in to his request.

Eve sidled close to Raider. "She must be one hell of a kisser."

"Shh."

Ramona broke away from her mystery lover and ran out of the stable. Raider listened as the man also fled. When they were out of the barn, Raider jumped up and ran to the loft gate. He peered out into the darkness, only to see two obscure figures running back toward the camp.

"Son of a bitch," he said. "I never did get a look at him. I wished he woulda talked louder."

When he turned back to find his clothes, Eve was putting a match to the wick of the lamp. "You ain't goin', are you, cowboy?"

Raider reached for his boots. "I got to go, honey. I got to see if I can find the man that was meetin' Ramona Masters. You sure you didn't recognize the voice?"

Eve shrugged. "Sounded soft. Had a little drawl. Coulda been anybody."

"Thanks, I couldn't tell that all by myself," he quipped.

"Hey!"

He looked over to see her legs spread wide.

"One more time?" she invited. "It won't take long. I got ways to make a man shoot when he thinks he's out of bullets."

"I bet you do."

Her thighs were so thick and dark. It wouldn't take that long, not really. Only long enough for him to miss a good clue.

"Sorry, honey."

Sometimes, he thought, you just had to take care of your duties.

Raider ran through the darkness, back toward the smell of smoldering campfires. Only a few lanterns burned in the encampment. Tired from the day's rehearsing, most of the performers had gone to bed.

Bull Harmon's light was out. So was the gas lamp in Henry Masters's wagon. Had Ramona slipped back into bed with him long enough to set right the argument from earlier in the evening?

Not a sound in the circus camp. Raider started back toward Augie's tent. He moved slowly, anticipating solid objects in the shadows. Something rustled to his left, behind iron bars.

Raider drew his Colt and aimed up at the ugly face that leered out at him in shadows. It looked like a deformed elk calf head bobbing on the end of an antelope's neck. Raider cried out and stepped back, thumbing the hammer of the Colt.

A loud bleating sound reverberated from the critter's slobbering mouth. The damn thing spit at him! If it hadn't been in the cage, Raider would have shot it. He came close.

"Dad-blamed smelly varmint!"

He did not have to look at the red stenciling on the rolling cage. Augie had been right. Raider knew a camel now that he was looking at it.

He caught his breath, holstered the Peacemaker, and started back for Augie's tent.

When he neared the wind-swelled dwelling, he saw that the candle had died. Augie was probably sleeping. Ilana should be safe. Unless Bull Harmon had been around.

Raider stepped to the tattered drape over the door. "Augie."

No response from the darkness.

Raider drew his gun. "Augie, if you're here, say somethin'."

He moved into the tent.

The scratching of a sulphur match in front of him. A circle of flame eased the darkness. Flame floating to the wick of the candle.

She leaned up on one arm and smiled at him. "You don't need that gun."

Raider lowered the Colt. "Sorry, Mrs. Masters. I wasn't exactly expectin' to find you here."

"Call me Ramona."

She threw her long legs over the edge of the cot, allowing them to fall out of her dress. Raider could not help but look. She caught him with her eyes and admonished him with a smile. Raider knew what she was doing. It made sense if she was the vixen everyone had made her out to be. He just hadn't expected it to come so soon.

He straighened his body. "Mrs. Masters, I don't think it's proper for you to be here. Where the devil is Augie, anyway?"

Ramona ignored him. She shook her hair and laughed. Her devastating eyes fell on the Colt again.

"That's lovely," she said. "May I see it?"

Raider scowled at her. "Mrs. Masters, I think the best thing for you to see is the inside of your husband's wagon."

She stood up, moving toward him. "Are you afraid of me, Raider?"

He shook his head. "No. But if your husband found us here together, he'd—"

"He'd believe exactly what I tell him," she replied.

Raider's eyes fell on her bosom. "Yeah, I reckon he would

at that. I reckon most men would step and fetch for a lady who looked like you."

She held out her slender hand. "Let me see your gun."

Raider decided to play it out. He emptied the cylinder of his Colt and gave it to her. "Take a good look," he said sarcastically.

Ramona raised a dark eyebrow. "Don't you trust me?"

"I trust you as long as I can see you."

She looked down the barrel of the Peacemaker. "People talk," she said. "You might have heard some unflattering things about me. Jealousy. This business is full of the green-eyed monster."

She aimed the barrel at Raider, swinging it suddenly. "And you've been talking to a lot of people, Mr. Pinkerton."

He snatched the gun away from her and then grabbed her wrist. "You'd better be going, Mrs. Masters."

"Ow," she said, wincing. "Let me go. I'll tell my husband that you tried to take advantage of me."

Raider pulled her toward the opening. "I don't care what you tell him. I just want you to clear out. But before you do, where's Augie and Ilana?"

"He took her back to her tent," she replied. "I made them go. Now unhand me, sir."

Raider let her go. She rubbed her wrist where he had grabbed her. Her chest heaved up and down.

"You'll pay for this."

"Clear out," he barked.

She moved closer to him, peering into his eyes. "No. It is you who should be on your way."

He met her hateful gaze with his black eyes. "How you figure?"

She pointed at him. "You have disrupted my show too much. A staging of this kind doesn't need someone snooping around. We take care of our own."

Raider grinned. "Did you take care of your husband's gold? In Kentucky?"

Her face went slack. "I don't know what you're talking about."

"No?"

"Get out," she railed. "My husband doesn't want you here. You almost cost him his best tent man, you ape."

"He pressed me," Raider said. "He had it comin'. By the way, you didn't meet him at the stable tonight, did you?"

She stepped backward, her hand at her throat. "Harmon is nothing. You have to leave. Henry said so."

Raider started past her.

"Where are you going?" she cried.

He looked back at her. "To ask Henry if he really wants me to leave."

"I speak for him," she said quickly.

Raider grinned. "When *he* tells me I'm finished, not before."

"No!" She hesitated. "Don't go. I'm sorry."

She began to cry, turning away from him, sobbing.

Raider did not buy it. "Come clean, Ramona. Tell me what you know about that robbery in Lexington. Tell me who you met in the stable tonight. What kind of game are you runnin' on Henry?"

She shook her head. "No, it's nothing like that. I . . . I don't know what to say."

"Tell me why you came here tonight."

She buried her face in a handkerchief. "To try to talk you into leaving. But not because I'm involved in any game on Henry. I love him, I realy do. I just lose patience."

"Why do you want me to leave?" he asked.

She spun toward him, grabbing his arms. "Don't you see. This is our last chance."

Raider pushed her away from him. "I heard that you gave Henry money. Where'd you get it?"

Her eyes were bulging. But she was quick with her answer. "There's a gentleman back in Atlanta. He sent me the money when Henry's gold was stolen."

His eyes narrowed. "This gentleman have a name?"

She nodded. "But I can't tell you who he is. It would ruin his reputation. You see, I wasn't married to him. I was his—"

"I don't care what you were to him," Raider replied, disgust evident in his voice. "I ought to take the truth to your husband right now."

"No!" Her voice trailed off, pitiful-like. "It would only break his heart. It might even kill him. This circus and me are all he has. If you take away either one, Henry will be lost."

Raider pointed a finger in her face. "I'm in this thing till the end, lady. If you're behind the stolen gold or the robbery in Lexington, I'm gonna find out. You understand? I ain't here to smoke out any gossip or to stomp around in anybody's married business."

She raised her hopeful eyes. "Then you won't tell Henry . . ."

"No promises," he replied. "Just go. If you're innocent, you ain't got a worry in the world."

She smiled. "Then I don't have a worry in the world, Mr. Raider. Good night. Sleep well."

She left without another word, easing into the shadows.

Raider exhaled. Ramona Masters was going to be a problem. Even if she was innocent, she would still cause complications. Had she really expected him to fall for the crying act? He had seen her cold, calculating manipulations. He had heard her calling her husband awful names. But was she capable of killing a man and engineering a gold theft? Raider wondered if Mr. Pinkerton had any men on the Lexington case.

Why, he asked himself, would somebody steal the gold a second time?

Too much confusion. He needed a drink. He started searching for the whiskey bottle he had drunk from earlier that day.

"Looking for this?"

Augie had come in the back way. He was holding the bottle in his tiny hand. His face was sad and drawn, his voice deflated.

Raider took the bottle and hit it strong. "How long you been standin' back there, Augie?"

"Too long. You weren't very respectful to Mrs. Masters."

Raider nodded. "But maybe she wasn't too respectful to me."

"She just wants to protect her show!" Augie cried.

"I hope you're right." He drank again.

Augie tried to keep defending his boss's wife. "She wants fame, Raider. That's all. How could she be involved in something like that robbery in Lexington? That man had his throat cut, the Wells Fargo agent, I mean."

Raider felt his own neck, remembering the way Ramona

had looked when she told him to sleep tight. "I ought to tell her husband that she's seein' somebody on the sly," he said finally.

Augie pointed a finger at him. "That's not true!"

Raider shrugged. "Don't believe me, then. Only she met him tonight at the stable. Ask the snake lady. We were there together."

"I will." Then he glared at the big man. "Are you going to tell Mr. Masters?"

Raider sighed deeply. "No. I mean, cheatin' wives may be against the Commandments, but nobody's gonna send Ramona to the territorial prison for diddlin' behind her hubby's back. Besides, he'll find out sooner or later. They always find out."

Augie was silent, almost like he was starting to believe it himself.

Raider patted the little man on the shoulder. "If she's guilty, I'll catch her. Otherwise, somebody else is behind all this bad-luck gold business. I don't like gold, Augie. It always causes . . . What the hell was that?"

Augie heard it too. A low wailing outside the tent, echoing through the night air. The noise grew louder, rising into the shrill cry of a nocturnal bird. It could have been a banshee howling over the plain.

Raider filled his hand with the Colt. "Somethin' else to worry about."

He pushed through the cloth door and leveled the Peacemaker at a man who sat cross-legged on the ground.

"Fair is foul and foul is fair!"

Raider lowered the Colt. "Hello, Professor. How you doin'?"

The old fortune-teller rose from the ground, swirling inside his black cape, pointing at Raider finally. "She has it now. But I fear she played most foully for it!"

The big man frowned. "Sounds like he's spoutin' that Shakespeare gibberish again."

"Desdemona was not unfaithful," Excalibur cried. "But Mrs. Ramona has sinned. Something is rotten. Frailty, thy name is woman. Out out, damned spot!"

Augie came up behind the big man. "The old boy is losin'

his mind," he said. "Can't tell the real world from the plays he's acted."

Excalibur straighted his body, lifting his hands to the sky. "Blow winds and crack your cheeks. Rage, you hurricanes!"

A spooky breeze rose suddenly on the plain, fluttering Excalibur's cape behind him. The big man shivered. It was almost like the professor had called up the wind.

Raider gestured toward Excalibur. "Maybe you oughta come in for a drink, Professor. We got some stew left if you—"

Excalibur pointed a finger at the Pinkerton. "Alas, poor Raider, I knew him, Horatio. A fellow of infinite . . . death!"

"Professor," Raider said, "don't be like that. Talk straight."

But Excalibur only turned away, dancing into the shadows, his cape swirling over him as he shouted broken lines from the Bard.

Raider still felt the coldness in his shoulders. "He's a real spook. I wonder if that's all an act to hide somethin' else?"

"I think he's really loco," Augie offered.

Raider shook his head. They went back into the tent, where the big man drank from the bottle of red-eye. There was nothing much for him to do. Just keep watching Bull Harmon and Ramona Masters. He'd just have to wait until they—or somebody else—tried something. Raider never liked waiting, but as it stood, patience seemed to be the only option.

CHAPTER ELEVEN

For the next week, Raider watched as the circus company settled into rigorous rehearsals. The unfortunate incidents upon his arrival were quickly forgotten by ardent professionals who were intent on giving the best possible performance. Even Bull Harmon kept a low profile. He worked as hard as any man Raider had ever seen, which almost made Raider respect him. If Harmon had not caused so much trouble beforehand, the baffled Pinkerton would not have kept him on the list of suspects in the gold theft.

When one section of the spectator's bleachers had been erected, Raider sat on the highest seat, watching day after day as the show took shape. He had to admit that Henry Masters possessed a real talent for staging. The short, cigar-chewing man with the derby strutted among his cast and crew, shouting orders that were obeyed instantly. He was constantly in a huddle with Jake Kelsey, discussing the order of events in the Wild West circus extravaganza.

Finally the finished program was established for the spectacular show. To begin on a light note, the circus parade would arrive first. Everyone in the company marched in a processional around the ring, with Jake Kelsey and the Georgia Nightingale riding on gilded white horses. As the parade exited, the clowns would stay behind and perform their comic antics until Ilana was ready to ride.

She was a thing of beauty, Raider thought. When she entered on the huge while stallion, he could not take his eyes off her. Her acrobatic talents on the back of the horse seemed to defy the very law of gravity itself. Flips. leaps, balancing, a handstand, rolls, somersaults—there seemed to be no end to her abilities. Just as Raider figured she would never top her last trick, Ilana brought out another move that completely astounded him.

At the end of her ride, Ilana always jumped from her horse, swinging in a circle to catch the tightwire above her. Then she would balance on the wire and go into a rope-walking act that even drew applause from those who had seen it countless times. No wonder Henry Masters had kept her on. She was practically a circus all by herself.

When the tightrope act was over, Ilana always found herself climbing down to a mock Indian invasion. Cast members dressed in full Indian battle regalia would enter to kidnap the young woman, thus bridging the circus with the Wild West show. After Ilana was dragged to center ring and tied to a stake, Cougar Kelsey made his entrance, hooting and swinging his pistols overhead, holding the reins of his palomino horse in his teeth. Using blank cartridges, Kelsey dispatched the Indians to their happy hunting ground, lifting Ilana onto his saddle when the bodies were strewn about at various intervals. Kelsey then rode out of the ring, waving, hopefully to the cheers of the audience.

Following the Indian war, five cowboys entered to perform rope tricks. They were competent, if not spectacular. Raider actually thought it was the most boring part of the show. Apparently Henry Masters felt the lull in the program, because he used a bronc ride immediately after the roping to liven things up.

When the bronc ride was over, the Georgia Nightingale made her entrance. She was pulled to center ring, looking angelic in a white dress, standing among fake flowers on the back of a decorated buckboard. She had a fair voice, Raider thought, suited to ballads and traditional ditties. She would not have been able to fill up a big opera house, but Raider doubted that her shortcomings amounted to much before a circus crowd.

The clowns came back after Ramona Masters, but only as a prelude to Jake Kelsey's second entrance. When a badman in black came out to menace the clowns, Cougar Kelsey was right there, fanning him down again with blank bullets. The clowns dragged the body out of the ring to allow Kelsey to go through his shooting tricks.

He blasted plates out of the air, cigarettes out of a clown's mouth, an apple off a young woman's head, and finally he mounted up to shoot the flying gourds on horseback. Raider would have been duly impressed had it not been for his knowledge of Kelsey's specially loaded cartridges. Still, the overall effect served Kelsey's image as the "World's Oldest Living Gunfighter." Raider felt certain that an unsuspecting audience would be adequately entertained.

After the first run-through by the troupe, Henry Masters turned and shouted to Raider, "What do you think, Mr. Detective?"

Raider tipped his hat and then began to applaud.

Masters laughed. "Let's hope the people of Kansas City feel the same way."

Raider spent some of his time outside the main arena. On the edges of the big show dwelled the marginal performers— the freaks, as one man put it. Raider had seen a carny-type setup before. Long rows of booths, some open, others guarded by curtains. Outside each booth stood a barker, the man who enticed unsuspecting suckers into the various sideshows.

On the day of the show, people could pay a penny or a nickle to see the tattooed man, the bearded lady, or Eve, the snake woman, with whom Raider enjoyed night after night of pleasure. Even the professor had shaped up into a pretty good magician. His hands were still quick for an old guy, making Raider wonder if he should have kept him on the list of suspects.

No, he decided finally, Ramona Masters would never have bedded down with a poor, wrinkled old codger like Excalibur.

Raider also found out that the sideshows had been allowed to stay on because Henry Masters payed them virtually nothing out of his own pocket. The novelty acts were supposed to collect their own money from the circusgoers and depending on the size of the crowd, times could be rich or lean. When Raider asked Eve why she stayed on with such a deal, she replied that Masters was more than fair. Some circus promoters demanded that the novelty acts pay them to ride along.

Staying outside the main arena allowed Raider to keep watch on Bull Harmon, who continued his hardworking ways. The chief roustabout was preparing to raise the big tent two days before the first scheduled performance. He didn't get out of line once as far as Raider could see. He had left Ilana alone, and he had stayed away from Ramona Masters, who was conducting herself like a saint. Raider had begun to doubt the suspected connection between Ramona and Harmon.

In fact, Raider was beginning to think his job was over. Without substantial clues there was no way to get a line on the missing gold. And Kelsey, who he had been sent to guard in the first place, was fine in all respects. Raider doubted if anyone—even himself—could get the drop on the leathery old buzzard.

Raider sighed as he watched the giant python slithering around Eve's shoulders. The big man really didn't want to leave. He was going to miss the nights above the stable in the loft. Eve was something to remember. Raider thought the circus life sort of agreed with him.

But what the hell was there to keep him in Kansas City?

When the big top was raised, Raider joined Augie on the highest seat in the risers. His black eyes scanned the taut canvas overhead. He shook his head, wondering how Bull Harmon could make so much cloth stand up with ropes and hardwood poles.

"Damned if it ain't somethin', Augie."

The little man nodded, his eyes riveted on the girl in the center ring. Ilana turned flip after flip on the back of a big white harness-bred. Raider focused his attention on the pretty bareback rider.

Augie smiled at the big man. "You're pretty stuck on Ilana, aren't you?"

Raider scowled at him. "What do you know about it?"

Augie shrugged. "I know that you visit the snake lady every night, but that you call out Ilana's name when you're sleeping in my tent."

"Really?" Then he shook his head. "You're puttin' me on."

"Don't be ashamed," Augie replied. "She's not too good for you."

"What makes you think—"

"You think that," the little man insisted. "I know you do. I've seen the way you look at her. You think she's too proper."

Raider exhaled and tipped back his Stetson. "Maybe I do. But there ain't nothin' gonna be done about it. You understand?"

Augie pointed to the ring. "Look out, here she comes."

Ilana dismounted at the bottom of the bleachers and waved to Raider. He waved back until she motioned for him to come down. Raider smiled and stepped carefully down the inclined bleacher seats.

"Hello," Ilana said sweetly. "How do I look in my new costume?"

She turned back and forth, displaying the rhinestoned leotard.

"You look okay," Raider replied, feigning indifference to the inspired curves of her supple body.

She waved a towel at him. "Oh, you silly!"

She leaned over closer to him. Raider expected something syrupy from her lips, a female sentiment. But Jake Kelsey called from behind, precluding the sweet declaration.

The World's Oldest Living Gunfighter was checking his special loads. "Ilana," he called. "Are you ready?"

She waved him off. "In a moment."

Raider eyed the gray-haired gunfighter. "What's that about?"

"A new trick," she replied nonchalantly. "I'm going to ride by Kelsey with a wooden pipe in my mouth. He's going to shoot the pipe as I ride by."

Raider bristled. "Ain't that a mite dangerous?"

She waved the towel at him again, flirting. "Don't be so afraid," she said coyly. "Kelsey is a professional. He knows what he's doing. If I thought I was in danger, I wouldn't do the trick."

How could he resist her perky manner? Maybe Augie was

right. Maybe he was sweet on Ilana. "Just be careful, little punkin."

She winked. "I intend to be. Otherwise I'll never get to make you my husband, Mr. Raider!"

"What?"

But she ran off to do the trick before Raider could offer further protestations. Raider despaired, realizing his earlier cautions had been correct. Women like Ilana expected more than he was capable of giving. And he was not going to take advantage of the situation, no matter how much that firm body excited him.

Ilana climbed on the broad back of the show horse and galloped past him as the horse turned in a circle. She waved to Raider and put the wooden pipe in her mouth. Jake Kelsey stood in the center of the ring, watching Ilana as she rode in the circle around him. His eyes carefully drew a bead on the wooden pipe, the target for his special loads.

Sweat broke out on Raider's brow. He did not like the look of the stunt at all. If Kelsey wavered, one of his special loads could blow off Ilana's pretty head.

Augie stepped up next to the big man. "What the heck is goin' on?"

Raider wiped his face with his bandanna. "New trick. Kelsey is gonna shoot that pipe out of Ilana's mouth."

Augie's eyes bulged. "While she's movin'?"

Raider nodded. "I don't like it. Hey, Jake," he called to the trick-shot artist, "do you really think this is somethin' you ought to try?"

But Kelsey did not hear him.

A crowd had gathered to watch the new stunt. Henry Masters was among the spectators. Raider appealed to Masters to stop Kelsey, but the promoter replied that the gunfighter knew what he was doing.

"Besides," Masters assured him, "the show needs a big finale. And it only looks dangerous."

Ilana went round and round on the horse.

Kelsey set his gunhand, waiting for the right moment.

Somewhere in the crowd there was a nervous drumroll.

Raider almost cried out as Kelsey drew his shooting iron.

The special loads exploded. Ilana's head did not even flinch as the pipe flew out of her mouth. Applause erupted from the members of the troupe. Augie and Masters clapped as well.

Raider only drew a breath of relief.

Ilana waved to him from the back of the horse, smiling and throwing kisses. Raider felt a twinge in his chest. Did he really love her? He didn't need complications like that.

He turned to Masters. "Beats anything I ever seen. You sure it's gonna be safe the next time?"

"Of course," the pudgy circus man replied. "And now that we have our big finish, we can open right on schedule. Two days, people," he called to the troupe. "Let's get to it."

There was a good feeling among the members of the cast. The show was finally ready. They only needed an audience to make it complete.

Raider nodded to Jake Kelsey. "Good shootin', Cougar. Keep it up."

Kelsey smiled. "Don't worry, big 'un. I ain't missed yet."

Ilana, who had dismounted, slipped next to Raider. "My tent, ten minutes," she said. Then she ran off before Raider could utter one word.

He shook his head. "Damned female."

Augie laughed at him. "Give up, Raider. You're bitten. And not by a snake, neither."

Raider figured it didn't matter. His circus duty would be over after the first performance. With things running so smoothly, he would no longer be needed. Masters would just have to say good-bye to his stolen money. Hell, with the Six-gun Circus in full swing, he was going to make so much money that he probably wouldn't miss his strongbox full of gold.

Raider sat back in the wooden chair, drinking from a glass of whiskey. "I still say you shouldn't do that stupid stunt, Ilana. It's too dangerous. I know about stuff like that. I been around guns for a long time. Do you hear me, honey?"

The pretty circus star languished on the opposite side of a silk screen, taking a hot bath. Raider had been in the chair trying to talk sense to her for almost half an hour. Ilana did not seem to be paying him much attention.

Raider kept on with his advice. "Kelsey is an old man,

honey. He's got his good days and his bad. Hell, if he misses, you could wind up without a head on your shoulders. You savvy?"

No reply. Was she just being stubborn? At least she could have the good manners to argue with him. After all, the only reason he had come to her tent was to talk some sense into her.

"Ilana, I think you ought to—"

Suddenly the petite bareback rider cried out, "Help me, Raider. Please. My God, no!"

The man from Arkansas came out of the chair, scuffling around the screen with his Colt drawn. He expected to find the worst. Instead, he found a naked, soapy, mischievous woman standing up in the tub. She flung her arms around his neck and began to lavish him with sudsy kisses.

Raider broke away and averted his eyes. "Are you crazy, woman? You're actin' like a plumb fool!"

She got out of the tub, sliding against him. "I love you, Raider. Don't you love me?"

He reached for a towel, wrapping it around her delicate frame. "It ain't important who loves who. You can't go around throwin' yourself at men like this. You could wind up in a lot of trouble."

Her lower lip extended in a pout. "It's Eve, isn't it? You love her and her snakes. Is that why you don't love me?"

Raider shook his head. "No, I don't love Eve."

She smiled. "Then you love me!"

He lowered his eyes. "Maybe," he said in a whisper.

Her towel hit the ground. "Then we can make love!"

Raider grabbed the towel and wrapped her in it again. "Look here, Ilana, you're a young woman. And I don't think it's right for a man like me to, you know, with a—"

"A virgin?" She laughed. "I am twenty-three. I know I look younger, but I am still a woman. And I am no virgin. I had a man, after my father died. He was my first. We were going to marry, but he was killed in a trapeze accident."

Raider blushed, not knowing what else to say.

Ilana stepped back and opened the towel. "Are you not pleased with me?"

Her diminutive form was perfectly proportioned. Smallish

breasts and hips, well-developed legs from riding, a sparse wedge of hair between her muscular thighs. Raider forced himself to look away.

She frowned. "You are not pleased."

"Ilana, we just can't. It wouldn't be right."

She started to cry. "You will not treat me as a woman. Then I will kill myself. I do not want to live if you will not make love to me."

Raider sighed. "Don't cry. Please don't cry."

But she would not stop sobbing. Raider finally wrapped her in his arms. She allowed the towel to fall, pressing her wet body against his.

"Come to bed with me," she whispered.

Raider looked down into her dark, teary eyes. "I can't marry you, Ilana. My work won't allow it."

She broke away, pulling him by the hand. "Then we will be husband and wife in spirit, until you leave."

"Ilana . . ."

The tears flowed more heavily. "No one loves me. I have felt so sad since my father died. Then you came to me. I am happy now. I want you, Raider. If only for a day, I want you."

He touched her soft cheek. "I want you too, honey."

He took her face in his hands, lowering his lips to her full mouth.

Ilana came to life, kissing him frantically. She helped him undress and then urged him toward her bed. Looking at her petite body spread out on the mattress, Raider thought she might shatter if he touched her. But she didn't. She sure as hell didn't.

They touched and kissed for a long time before he entered her. Ilana responded with a surprising deftness. They kept at it for the rest of the afternoon, until the sun had fallen below the horizon.

When they were finished, she rolled his limp manhood between her tiny fingers. "You are much bigger than my other lover. I may be too sore to ride tomorrow."

A pained look came over Raider's countenance.

She laughed. "I am only teasing you. You were wonderful. And . . . .I love you, Raider."

He sighed. "I reckon I love you too, Ilana."

He wondered if he had made a mistake. Young women

could sometimes let their imaginations get the best of them. Would she want him to remain and be her husband? Raider could not imagine himself staying on with Masters and company, despite his growing affections for Ilana and the circus.

"I am so happy," she said. "The show is going well. My new trick will bring down the house."

Raider raised himself on one elbow. "Ilana, let's talk about that stunt. I don't think you ought to go through with it. It's too dangerous."

She giggled. "Already you are fussing over me like a concerned husband."

The impatience crept into Raider's voice. "Don't change the subject. I'm tryin' to tell you not to put your life in danger."

She rested her fingers on his lips, assuring him that everything would be fine. There was no danger. None at all.

Raider kept up his argument until she persuaded him to make love to her again.

And by the time he was able to resume his words of warning, Ilana was snoring lightly on his thick chest.

CHAPTER TWELVE

Opening night for the Six-gun Circus!

Flyers had been distributed, and the posters had been dated and tacked up all over Kansas City. Although the first performance had been scheduled for seven o'clock that evening, people began to arrive as early as four. The games of chance and the sideshows opened early to take advantage of the eager crowd. While hundreds fed the carnys their hard-earned coins, another throng chose to eat picnic suppers on the grounds around the main tent.

Raider used the time before the show to thoroughly check the wings of the big top for any signs of trouble. The backstage mill was in motion, with cast and crew hurrying about in last-minute confusion. Still, there didn't seem to be any tension or complication beyond opening night jitters.

Raider felt a sense of relief. He wanted the show to succeed. Over the weeks he had acted as security for the circus, he had come to know and like many of the performers, as well as Masters and Kelsey. Even Ramona had tempered her cheating nature, sticking close to her husband when she wasn't singing.

So the big man went through his tasks with a bored professionalism. His black eyes scrutinized every little detail no matter how insignificant or irrelevant it might seem. He could not find a thing out of place. Right before the curtain, he checked in with Henry Masters, who seemed relaxed.

The star of the show, Cougar Jake Kelsey, World's Oldest Living Gunfighter, had put on his shiny monkey suit. He was a picture of calm, standing next to the white horse he would ride in the circus parade. Cougar Jake twirled twin .45s on his fingers, anticipating his lead-flying act.

Raider tipped back his hat, peering down at Masters. "Dog me if I can spot any trouble, Mr. Masters."

The cigar-chewing showman had abandoned his derby and tweed suit to dress up in a ringmaster's costume, complete with cane, high hat, and black tails. "Good job, Raider. Sorry you couldn't find my gold."

"I might want to ask you a few more questions after the show, Mr. Masters."

The ringmaster's eyes narrowed. "Oh?"

"Don't get excited," Raider replied. "There's just a few loose ends I got to clear up. Mr. Pinkerton is gonna make me write some kinda report on this, and I want it to be right. If you could help me, I'd be much obliged."

Masters just nodded and turned his attention back to the show.

Raider wondered if he would really be able to put his mind to rest. He wasn't used to ending up in a dead-end box canyon. He supposed the nagging feeling would be something that he had to learn to live with.

Would Doc have been able to get to the bottom of things? he wondered.

A blast from several brass horns called his attention to the circus tent. The big top had been done up with all the trimmings. Red, white, and blue streamers were strung from all angles, hanging from the fan-shaped banners that patriotically depicted the colors of the flag. Torches and gas lamps illuminated the oval of the center ring. Masters had even hired the four-piece band to enliven the atmosphere with festive music.

Raider shook his head in admiration. "I got to hand it to ole Masters," he said to himself. "He really knows how to pitch a wingding."

He felt a tugging on his trousers.

"Howdy, Augie."

The little man held up a note. "From Ilana."

Raider hesitated before he unfolded the perfumed paper. *I love you* were the only words printed in her delicate hand. Raider felt his stomach churning. He was still worried about the trick-shot finale, even though Kelsey had been reassuring him that the stunt was safe.

But what could he do? Nothing more than find a seat. When he was in the top row of the riser, he sat back and watched the crowd.

The music seemed to draw them in. More tickets had been sold than there were seats, so a standing area was quickly cleared. Masters wanted every dime he could get. With the Georgia Nightingale in tow, Raider was sure that Masters was going to need it.

Raider had decided to tell Masters his doubts about Ramona. He didn't care if Masters blew up or if Allan Pinkerton demanded his head in a noose. He was going to come clean with the truth, no matter who got hurt.

The music swelled and finally died.

Dressed in a top hat and tails, holding a silver megaphone, Henry Masters proceeded to the podium at the center of the ring. "Ladies and gentlemen, tonight you are going to witness one of the historic spectacles of all time. The one, the only Six-gun Circus!"

The spectators cheered. The band started up again. Henry had them whipped up into a frenzy, ready for anything. They rose to their feet when the colorful circus parade entered from the wings.

Raider focused on a certain young bareback rider who made her entrance standing on the broad shoulders of a white horse. Her sequined costume glittered in the torchlight. She blew a kiss into the stands when she passed Raider's section.

It was going to be tough to leave her. His little romance had gotten to him more than he would ever have guessed it could. He should have stayed with the snake lady, he thought. Eve wouldn't even talk to him after he took up with Ilana. He had never been able to handle more than one woman at a time.

The Georgia Nightingale passed by, waving to the crowd from the seat of a buckboard. Did Raider detect the slightest smirk on her lips? She was probably glad to be rid of him. He watched as the columns of circus people completed the circle around the tent.

When the parade had disappeared into the wings, the clowns went to work. Augie fussed over some of the younger children in the front tow, tossing them sugar candy. He made funny faces and turned somersaults to make them laugh.

Suddenly a gasp went through the crowd, forcing the clowns to give way to the next attraction—Ilana had made her entrance atop the huge show horse. The audience, like the big Pinkerton, could not keep their eyes off her. Each trick brought a bigger round of applause. They came up off their seats when she swung onto the high wire. She had a lovely smile on her lips. She was perfect, and the spectators loved her for it.

Her wire-walking titillated the crowd until the mock Indian invasion thundered from the wings. When Ilana was sufficiently captured, Cougar Kelsey made his entrance accompanied by a flourish from the band. Whoops and cheers resounded as he rescued Ilana from the burning stake. He lifted her onto the saddle in front of him and then exited on the palomino.

Loud applause called them both back for a bow.

Next, the trick ropers came on. They were mildly amusing, but the bronc ride really enlivened the audience and readied them for the Georgia Nightingale.

At first they seemed to adore Ramona Masters. She cooed from the back of the buckboard, her voice in good pitch. But during the third song, a few disgruntled boos were heard and someone shouted, "Bring back the cowboy and the girl!" Ramona never wavered, finishing her entire program as if nothing had happened, singing to an audience who did not want to hear her.

Raider shook his head. He could not believe that Masters had let her go on. She wasn't really much of a draw compared to the rest of the show. Love could do a damned sight to make a man's head as muddy as a clay-flooded creek. Things might change after Raider told Masters the truth about his young wife.

Cheers rose again when the clowns ushered in Cougar Jake. The old boy fanned down the man in black and set to blasting clay gourds out of the air. When the gourds burst, confetti exploded under the torchlight. The crowd ate it up, hollering for more.

Raider's stomach began to churn, as he knew what was coming next.

Henry Masters stepped up onto his platform near the center ring. He lifted his hand and shouted, "Tonight you will see a death-defying thrill never before witnessed west of the Mississippi—or anywhere else in the entire world."

Loud cheers and catcalls from the hungry spectators.

Ilana burst from the wings, standing on the white horse, the wooden pipe sticking out of her mouth.

Raider still didn't like it one damned bit.

Kelsey stepped down off the palomino and strode to the center of the ring with his special gun in hand.

Masters continued to whet their appetites. "Ladies and gentlemen, as you can see, the little lady is holding a pipe in her mouth as she circles around Cougar Jake Kelsey, World's Oldest Living Gunfighter and Marksman Extraordinaire." His voice dropped a solemn octave. "Please, we ask that you remain silent while Cougar Jake concentrates on his task. Do not talk, do not move, do not breathe. A human life hangs in the balance. Cougar!"

Kelsey squared his shoulders.

Ilana held the circle well, running in a tight pattern around Kelsey. Raider sat forward on the edge of the bleacher. His heart was racing.

The audience drew a breath as Kelsey's hand fell toward his gun.

Raider stood up.

Kelsey drew and fired.

Ilana's body buckled suddenly and she fell to the ground.

A stunned audience stared at her tiny figure lying in the dirt.

Masters was the first one to reach her. He looked down and then raised his megaphone. "She's all right, folks. Just part of the show." He motioned for the band to start playing again.

Raider ran down the bleachers, bolting out of the stands. He lifted Ilana in his arms and carried her to the wings, all to the cheers of an unsuspecting crowd. He eased her onto a cot in her dressing room.

Blood oozed from a hole in Ilana's chest.

"My God," Raider said.

Augie was right beside him. "What happened?"

Raider looked away from the lifeless body. "She'd dead. Somebody shot her. In the heart."

Kelsey rushed in with Masters beside him.

"Is she all right?" asked the aging shootist.

Raider shook his head. "No. She's gone." He was trying his damnedest not to cry.

Master's hands were trembling. "Damn it all, Kelsey, you should have been more careful with those confounded pistols."

Kelsey gaped with horror at Ilana's body. "I didn't mean to do it. I aimed straight, just like in practice."

Raider put his hand on Kelsey's shoulder. "You didn't kill her, Jake."

Kelsey stared glassy-eyed at the big Pinkerton. "What are you saying?"

Raider fought to maintain his last shreds of professional conduct. He could barely get out the words. "She was killed by a small-caliber weapon. Jake was shooting his special loads. If he had hit her with one of his shots, I can't even think of what she would . . ." The words caught in his throat.

Masters fumbled to light his cigar. "In God's name, why would someone want to kill Ilana?"

Raider swallowed the grief that burned inside him. "She's gonna have a proper funeral," he said bitterly. "I want all of you there. We're gonna find a church and a preacher to say words over her. I ain't ashamed to say I loved that little girl."

Masters nodded. "Anything you say, Raider."

The big man's eyes were circles of black. "And after the funeral, I'm comin' back here and I'm gonna find out who did this thing." He turned toward the performers who had gathered outside the dressing room. "I'm comin' back, you all hear that? And I'm gonna find the murderer. And I don't care who it is, I'm gonna kill him. Is that understood?"

Someone in the gathering replied, "Amen to that, brother. Amen to that!"

"All right," Raider said, "I think I got it set up the way it was last night. Y'all sit tight while I study on it."

Raider focused his intense gaze on the center ring. He hadn't said much since the funeral that morning. He was hurting inside, but he was not going to let up until he found the person who had killed Ilana.

The Pinkerton had decided to reenact the moments just before Ilana's untimely death. Raider stood in the same spot where Kelsey had fired his one shot. Augie sat on a horse to simulate Ilana's position just as the real death bullet was fired. Behind Augie rested the ringmaster's raised podium, where Masters had announced the fatal finale.

Augie raised his hands into the air. "Raider, you want me to stand up on the horse's back like Ilana?"

Raider shook his head. "No. Just sit tight. Let me take it from here. Now, Kelsey raised his gun . . . Boom! He fired. Let's see if he hit his mark."

Raider walked past the show horse, and paced back a few steps, scanning the ground. After a couple of minutes he reached down and lifted the front half of a wooden pipe. He held it up for Augie to see.

"I'll be damned," the little man said.

Raider nodded. "Kelsey was straight on target."

Augie scratched his head. "Then who killed Ilana?"

Raider looked toward the bleachers. "Somebody fired from another position. They knew Kelsey's shot was comin', so they hid up and waited for the chance to fire. Probably there, under the seats."

Augie clapped his hands together. "Yes, that's it!"

Raider hurried over to the risers, looking until he found the correct angle. "Here," he said. "There's powder burns where the killer rested a gun." Raider took aim with the imaginary weapon. His head bobbed up quickly.

"That's it," he cried.

Augie frowned. "What is it?"

"The angle," Raider replied. "I can see it clear. Ilana was in line with Master's podium when the shot was fired from under the seats. She wasn't too lucky, but she sure as hell saved the ringmaster."

Augie gaped at the big Pinkerton. "You think somebody was really tryin' to shoot Henry Masters?"

Raider came out from behind the bleachers. "Who would

want to kill a young woman like Ilana? She didn't have a soul in this world who hated her."

"What about Bull Harmon?" Augie asked.

"I think he wanted somethin' else," Raider replied. "No, I'm bettin' that Masters was the real target."

Raider and Augie both looked up.

Augie peered toward the dressing area. "What was that?"

"Two gunshots," Raider replied, reaching for his Colt.

"Might be Kelsey practicin'," Augie offered.

"Might not be, neither."

A caped figure shot through the shadows of the backstage area. Raider caught a glimpse of the furling cloth as it flashed past an opening in the tent. The man seemed to be carrying a pistol in his right hand.

"The professor," Augie cried. "I'd know that cape anywhere."

Raider held up the Peacemaker. "Looks like Excalibur has finally gone loco."

Raider started after the fluttering cape. He lost him somewhere backstage. He hurried for the professor's tent. Excalibur wasn't there. Where the hell had he gone? Surely he couldn't run that fast. He was an old codger, after all. Where? He was running wild asses all over the camp.

Two more gunshots in the distance.

Raider started running. It wasn't hard to find the source of the shooting. The crowd had already gathered by the time Raider arrived at Jake Kelsey's wagon. Cougar Jake stood over the bleeding body of Professor Excalibur. The old gunfighter held two smoking Colts in his hands.

"I had to do it," Kelsey said sadly. "He was runnin' straight at me with that gun."

Raider reached down, lifting Excalibur's cape away from his body. Two loads of lead had obliterated the old man's feeble chest. Raider had to look away. Kelsey's special bullets had done a job on the late fortune-teller.

Kelsey holstered his Colts. "I reckon he finally went over the cliff."

Raider nodded and exhaled. "Yeah, we saw him runnin' around backstage. He was packed and ready for somethin'."

Someone behind them shouted, "Look! In his hand!"

Raider bent down and opened the professor's cold fingers. Two gold coins fell onto the ground. Double eagles, the same kind of currency that Masters had lost in the robbery.

Kelsey peered at the double eagles. "If he was the thief, then we should find the rest of the gold in his tent."

"Unless he spent them," Raider offered.

Kelsey waved him off. "Where would an old man like that spend five thousand dollars? Come on, let's go have a look at his things."

But as he started off, a shrill cry resounded from the opposite direction.

Raider cradled the butt of his Peacemaker. "What now?"

A woman screamed at the top of her lungs. The crowd parted to let her run forward. Ramona Masters had a hysterical look in her eyes.

"Henry!" she cried. "Dead!" She pointed at Excalibur's body. "He shot my Henry. He killed him!"

"I'll have a look," Raider said. "Kelsey, you check Excalibur's tent."

In a few minutes both Raider and Kelsey came back.

Kelsey nodded. "Gold's in the professor's tent. Is Henry . . ."

Raider lowered his head. "Dead. Shot twice in the chest. I reckon it was the professor who killed him after all."

Mrs. Masters broke down sobbing. Augie stroked her hair. She wrapped her arms around the little man.

Raider glared at her. Were the tears an act? She had everything now, the gold and the circus. Would she continue to cry until she was alone?

No one noticed the sly tilt to Raider's countenance as he asked Augie to help him with the body of Henry Masters.

"I'm staying with Miss Ramona," Augie snapped. "She needs me."

Ramona looked up, her face tear-streaked. "No, Augie. Please help Mr. Raider." She stood straight, peering out over the troupe. "I want all of you to know that the circus will go on. I think Henry would have wanted it that way."

"I'll bet," Raider muttered under his breath. "Come on, Augie. We have to take Henry Masters to the undertaker."

The little man came along quietly. They hurried to Henry

Masters's wagon to retrieve the body. Raider had to slow down so Augie could keep up with him.

"You don't look sad enough," Augie accused.

Raider just kept quiet.

Augie shook his head. "What a crazy way for things to end. That old man going off his rocker. Isn't that right, Raider? Raider? Isn't this a crazy way for things to end?"

The big man was staring straight ahead with a distant gleam in his eyes. "Crazy, Augie? Maybe. But I got me a feelin' that things are gonna get a lot more loco in a hurry. Yep, little friend, somethin' tells me that the lunacy is just beginnin'."

Augie thought about the big Pinkerton's bizarre comment as they loaded Henry Masters's limp body onto the back of a buckboard. How could things get started if it was all over? Hadn't Excalibur been the thief and the killer after all? An old loon who waded out too far into the current.

Tears gathered in Augie's eyes. Raider drew the sheet over Henry Masters. There didn't seem to be much pity or remorse in Raider's eyes.

"You don't even care that Henry's dead!" Augie accused, pointing a tiny finger at the big man.

Raider grabbed him and swung him onto the seat of the buckboard. "Don't mark me up short, Augie."

Raider hopped up beside him and took the reins. "Better let me handle the wagon, Augie."

The little man snatched the reins away. "No! I'm going to drive the wagon. I get more practice than you anyway."

Raider gave in. They started for town on the main road, bumping along at a slow pace. When they were out of sight, away from the circus camp, Raider suddenly grabbed the reins and steered the horse off the road.

Augie gawked at the big man. "What's wrong with you?"

Raider replied with a declamation that had helped him with the late Professor Excalibur. "There's method to my madness." He still wondered what the hell that meant.

At the same stable he had shared more than once with the snake lady he reined back on the team horse. He climbed down and threw back the sheet that covered the ringmaster's body. "Come on down here and give me a hand, Augie."

The dwarf folded his runty arms. "No. You're sick. You ought to be locked up. I'd kill you if I had a gun."

Raider grabbed him and pulled him down.

"Have some respect for the dead," Augie cried.

But Augie helped him carry the body into the stable. They stretched Masters out on a pile of hay.

Raider pointed toward a dried clump on the stable floor. "Fetch that for me, Augie."

The little man grimaced. "But that's shit!"

"Just do it."

Augie reluctantly obeyed him, fetching the manure but then throwing it at Raider's feet. The big man picked up the dung and began to wave it under the nose of Henry Masters.

Augie thought he was crazy. "Since when is shit a cure for gunshot wounds?"

Raider ignored him, keeping the chip balanced under the circus promoter's red nose.

Augie jumped back, emitting a sharp cry.

Suddenly Masters had jerked, stirring back into life with a jolt.

Augie's eyes bulged. "What did you do to him?"

"He wasn't dead," Raider replied. "Come on, Henry, wake up. Augie, see if you can find us a bucket of water."

Augie, glad to have his boss alive, sprang quickly to the task. When he brought back the water, they worked on Masters for a while, dabbing his head with a wet cloth and tending two large bruises on his chest. After an hour or so, Masters began to come out of his sleep. He opened his eyes and gaped up at the big Pinkerton who hovered over him.

Masters cried out and bolted upright into a sitting position.

"Easy," Raider urged. "You just been out for a while. You're still livin', Mr. Masters."

The ringmaster rubbed his eyes. "Where am I? Oww... there's a pain in my chest. Damn, it hurts."

Raider handed him a dipper of water. "Here. Take a little drink."

Masters scoffed at the water. "I want something stronger than that."

The resurrected promoter reached into his coat pocket and pulled out a small flask of whiskey. He took a long drink and offered the flask to Raider. The big man shrugged it off, even though he wanted a strong belt. He had to stay sharp because things were going to get hairy real soon.

"What the devil is going on here?" Masters asked.

Raider forced him to lie back on the straw. "You just take it easy, Mr. Masters. I want you to think back and see if you can tell me what you remember right before you were shot."

"Shot?" Masters's eyes rolled around for a moment. "I was in my office," he said finally. "And I was having a drink with Ramona. Then I felt sick to my stomach." He wiped his hand across his sweaty forehead. "I'm still woozy. My eyes seemed to cloud up."

"Go on."

"A hand," Masters said. "I saw a hand coming out of the blur. There was a gun. And a cape. The professor's cape. It was him."

"Did you see his face?" Raider asked.

Masters shook his head. "No." After a moment he touched his chest. "Why wasn't I killed by those gunshots?"

Raider reached into his vest pocket and pulled out two cartridges. "I took these blanks out of the gun I found in Excalibur's hand after he supposedly shot you. They're blank loads. Like the ones used in the fake Indian fight. They make a lot of noise, but they aren't lethal."

The pain in Masters's chest felt lethal enough. "If they're blanks, how come I'm hurt?"

"Close range," Raider replied. "The wadding got you. Somebody fired pretty close to make sure you were dead."

"Excalibur," Masters said under his breath.

"Maybe," Raider said. "Maybe not. But that's what I want to find out."

Masters tried to get up. "I'm going back there at once and get to the bottom of this. Oww."

Raider finally made him lie back and drink some water. "Look here, Henry, I took you out of there so everyone would believe that you had been killed."

"Why?"

Raider exhaled. "Because it's time to catch the person behind all this. We'll move tomorrow, after the performance. It won't take a whole lot to set it up, but we still have to be careful."

Masters smiled weakly. "Good thinking, Raider. Although I wish you would go back and stay with Ramona. She might be in danger."

He saw Raider and Augie exchange doleful glances.

"What is it?" he asked. "What are you holding back from me, Raider?"

The big man lowered his eyes. "It's about your wife, sir. I think it's time you heard some truth for a change."

"Don't start with that nonsense!" Masters cried.

Augie put his hand on his boss's shoulder. "Listen to him, Mr. Masters. He's telling you straight out. And I can back him up."

Raider explained everything in a flat voice. Ramona's liaison with another man, her visit to Raider's tent, the resentment of her by the other members of the company.

Masters seemed to sink back into the haystack as he heard it all.

Raider sighed. "We also think she may have been involved with that Wells Fargo job in Lexington. Ain't it true that she gave you money when you needed it?"

Masters glanced away. "She said it came from her uncle in Savannah."

"He ain't her uncle," Raider replied. "Even if she did get the money from him."

Augie pointed up at the big man. "You're forgetting one thing. They found Mr. Masters's gold in Excalibur's tent."

"Planted there," Raider offered. "Either somebody put Excalibur up to it or they faked it so they could make it look like the professor was killin' Henry. Only they picked up the wrong gun, one with blanks."

"I saw Excalibur," Masters insisted.

"Really? You saw his cape. But you said yourself that your eyes was all fuzzy. It coulda been anybody. Even . . . even your wife."

The circus promoter glared up at Raider. "I hate you, cowboy. I hate you if you're wrong, I hate you if you're right. I love Ramona."

Raider gestured back toward the big top. "Then ride on into camp and see how she greets you. See if she's happy to see you alive."

"And if I don't?" Masters barked gruffly.

Raider half smiled. "Then we catch the weasel in the chicken coop."

Masters stared up at the ceiling. "If she's guilty, my whole life is ruined anyway." He took a deep, painful breath. "Then we do it your way, Raider."

The big man nodded.

"Only, if Ramona is innocent," Masters added, "I have a pair of dueling pistols in my wagon. I won't hesitate to use them."

Raider wondered if the pudgy man could really shoot. He had sure lowered the boom on the showman. Masters looked stunned. Those two blank wads in his chest hadn't helped much.

Raider thought about the whiskey in Masters's coat pocket.

But instead of drinking, he began to outline his plan to catch Ramona Masters's accomplice.

CHAPTER THIRTEEN

The following night, a memorial performance of the Six-gun Circus was presented in honor of the late ringmaster, Henry Masters. Again the good citizens of Kansas City turned out in droves. Masters stood beside Raider, watching from the stable as the eager spectators made their way to the big tent. Augie, who had gone into camp to enact Raider's plan, had come back with the information that Ramona Masters was to play the ringmistress in the wake of her husband's ill-fated departure.

The promotor sighed, his face drawn and cold. "I'm not even in the ground yet and she's open for business."

Raider said nothing.

Masters turned toward the big man. "Do you really think this scheme will come off like you planned?"

Raider shrugged. "Nothin' is foolproof, Henry. Just be patient. It'll come to us if we wait. You can wait a while longer to learn the truth."

Masters replied that the truth was the only thing he feared.

Across the plain, in the widening shadows, the circus band wailed again under the big top. They were going through everything but the bareback and high wire acts—Ilana's specialties. In addition to acting as the ringmistress, Ramona Masters had inserted herself into the role of damsel-in-distress, allowing Kelsey to rescue her from the perils of the mock Indian battle.

All of this they were told by Augie, who had to be back in time for his clowning.

As the show raged on, Masters would not relinquish all hope for his wife's innocence. "I'll bet he's making her do this," he said thoughtfully. "Harmon is forcing her to go through with it."

Raider just leaned back against the wall. "I reckon we'll see."

His plan had been a simple one. He had sent a message to all the likely men in the show: *We are not free of him yet. Trouble. Tonight at the stable. Be careful, my love.* The snake lady, with a little coaxing from Augie, had penned the notes, which would no doubt upset a few circus wives. But Raider was assuming that Ramona knew well enough to play at grief for a while before she took up with her accomplice. The note would smoke him out. He could not resist a quick rendezvous, especially with the threat of trouble.

But they still had to wait.

Inside, the circus laughter rose and fell. Applause. Masters sank lower into his depths. If he had really been dead, Ramona was as much as dancing on his grave. A hateful squint appeared on his face, and it did not go away.

"Easy boy," Raider warned. "We're gonna need clear heads for this thing."

"Give me a gun," Masters commanded.

Raider waved him off. "I'll handle the fireworks if need be. You just be ready to surprise the hell out of somebody who ain't expectin' to see you."

Masters clenched his teeth. "I'll see that Harmon never works in another circus as long as he lives."

The applause rose and died for the last time. Inside the tent, Kelsey had gone through the pipe trick with another young girl in a shiny leotard. This time the girl was standing still instead of riding on a moving horse. Gradually the crowd filed away, going merrily to their mounts and buggies. Some were on foot, and a few fancy carriages were making for home.

"Good crowd," Masters said ironically. "I should die every day."

It was almost midnight before the final carriage lamp disappeared down the road. Another hour passed as the lights died out in the circus camp. A bright moon rose overhead, making it easy for clown-faced Augie to find his way back to the stable. Raider lifted him up into the hayloft and then climbed back up himself.

The big man checked his Colt. He also had a shiny new Winchester for real persuasion. He leaned back in the shadows with the rifle in hand.

"Raider," Augie started, "can you . . . "

The big man urged him to keep his voice low. Boots rustled gravel outside the stable. The boots came closer, pausing at the entrance. Slow sliding and creak of the stable door. They saw his frame in the moonlight. He stepped in and hesitated in the shadows.

"Ramona, are you here?"

Raider recognized the voice immediately. He had heard it before, that night when he and the snake woman had shared the same loft. Raider reached for a match in his vest pocket.

"Ramona," the shadowy suitor said below, "don't play games with me. Come out. You know how much I love you. Please."

Raider struck the match, holding it up for a second before he torched the wick of a coal-oil lantern.

The man below snapped up his head. "Who's there?" he cried.

Raider raised the lantern. "It's me." He swung the light to his left. "And Henry Masters."

They saw him clearly in the orange flame.

"Masters!" he cried, eyes wide. "But the professor killed you!"

"I'm here," Masters replied. "The professor picked up the wrong gun. He tried to kill me with blanks."

The man's hand fell toward the Colt at his side.

Raider levered the Winchester. "Don't try it, boy."

The man froze, his hand over the butt of the pistol.

Raider waved the barrel of the rifle. "I don't want to kill you, hombre. Augie's gonna come down and take those two hog-legs. Go on, Augie."

The little man climbed down the ladder, stepping toward the man in the white Stetson.

Raider smiled, shaking his head. "I got to hand it to you, boy. You sure had us fooled. Who woulda thunk it?"

Masters scowled as Augie removed the ivory-handled Colts from the man's double holsters. "I can't believe she would be involved with him. He's old enough to be her grandfather."

"And you're only old enough to be her father," Raider replied. "Augie, take Mr. Kelsey's guns outside and hide 'em someplace. Then, old feller, you got a lot of explainin' to do."

"I don't reckon I have much choice," replied the World's Oldest Living Gunfighter. He glared at Raider. "You're a mighty big man with that rifle on me, Arkansas. Maybe you'd give me a chance straight on sometime. Man to man, six-gun to six-gun."

Raider shrugged. "It might come to that, but I doubt it. You're in custody now, Kelsey."

Augie came back into the stable. "Guns are hidden."

Raider pointed to a piece of rope that hung on the wall. "Now tie his hands behind him, Augie."

Kelsey remained extremely calm as he was bound. He finally sat back on the straw, half smiling. "I don't know what I done is a crime," he offered. "It's not right with the laws of God, but I—"

Masters pointed a finger at his partner. "Shut him up, Raider!"

"No," the big man replied. "I want him to keep talkin'."

And Kelsey did talk—for a long time.

Raider eyed him cautiously, wondering if he could believe what he had just heard. He tipped back his Stetson, exhaling. "Cougar, you tell us you're in love with Ramona, but then you deny havin' anythin' to do with the gold theft in Lexington, or tryin' to kill Henry."

Kelsey nodded sincerely. "I keep tellin' you, Ramona and I were carryin' on. She said she loved me. Hell, why do you think I put up my own money to help save this show?"

Raider leaned forward, his eyes narrow. "And you never tried to take over the circus? Never tried to help her kill her husband?"

"I never helped her hurt no one," Kelsey replied, his tone pleading. "I never wanted to kill anybody, not even that crazy magician. But hell, he was runnin' straight for me, comin' on, wavin' that gun. I didn't know he had blanks in it."

Raider shook his head. "I don't know, Cougar. I'd like to believe you. Ramona does seem to have a powerful sway with the gentlemen."

"I never wanted to fall for that chippy!" Kelsey declared.

Masters snarled at him, "Watch your mouth."

Raider kept after the old cowboy. "You don't know nothin' about that gold turnin' up in the professor's tent? Or Ilana gettin' killed?"

Kelsey hung his head. "God help me if I do."

"And you don't know if Ramona was in on that Lexington job?"

Kelsey gaped in disbelief. "How could she?"

"Then where'd she get that gold she gave Henry? The gold that was stolen later from you!"

"I gave it to her," Kelsey replied. "It was my life savings. Except for what I gave Henry to buy in for half. I gave it all to her, then she wanted me to watch over it. It's mixed up. Hell, I'm so sweet on her, I'd do about anything she asked."

"What about you bein' hit over the head?" Raider asked.

Kelsey shrugged. "That really happened. I was movin' that strongbox back to my wagon when somebody cold-cocked me."

Masters glared at the World's Oldest Living Gunfighter. "Do you mean to say you never tried to help Ramona take my circus away from me?"

Kelsey shook his head. "No, sir. Not even when she said things might be easier if you weren't here. I never took that talk serious."

Raider chortled. "He could be tellin' the truth. Kelsey, you know if Ramona was foolin' around with anybody else in the show?"

Kelsey lowered his head again. "I think there was two or three of them."

Masters gave an anguished cry. "Give me a gun, I'm going to kill this old fart."

Raider had to restrain him.

"I'm sorry," Kelsey said with real sorrow in his voice, "but it's true. That's why I was so dad-blamed jealous."

"Bull Harmon," Masters blurted out. "Was he one of her lovers?"

"He wanted to be," Kelsey replied. "I don't know if he was or not. She was usin' him for somethin'."

Raider nodded. "So that's why you wanted to have Harmon fired." His brow fretted. "But if Harmon was so hot for her, why didn't he come runnin' when Augie delivered the note?"

Kelsey looked dumbfounded. "What note?"

Augie jolted to attention. "By golly, Raider, I never delivered a note to Kelsey here. I took one to Harmon and all the others. But not Cougar Jake. Remember, we decided he was too old."

Raider felt a sourness in his stomach. "I guess he ain't too old. Kelsey, how the hell did you end up here?"

"Ramona told me to come," Kelsey replied. "She said to meet her here after the show."

Raider slammed his fist into his palm. If Harmon had gotten his note, he must have gone straight to Ramona Masters. Which meant that they were both on to Raider's plan.

The big man was angry. "We've been fooled. We trapped the wrong weasel."

Kelsey struggled to his feet. "I'm awful sorry, but she's just the kind of woman who's hard to resist."

Masters dropped his eyes and nodded. "I know, Mr. Kelsey. I know." He glared at Raider. "I say we take this straight to my wife. I want to hear what she has to say."

"You and me both," Raider replied. "Let's get to it."

They started off without Kelsey. He took a few steps after them. "Hey," called the old shootist, "don't leave me."

Raider looked over his shoulder. "We'll be back for you."

Cougar Jake had a sorrowful look in his gray eyes. "But I want to do right by Mr. Masters. I want to help. I want to make good."

Masters looked at Kelsey. "What do you think, Raider?"

The big man exhaled. "Well, he did fess up. I leave it to you, Masters. Just be quick."

After a moment of thought, Masters nodded. "You can come, Kelsey. But no gun. You stay back. If there's trouble, you make for town to get the police. And Augie, you go to your tent when we get into camp. I don't want you gettin' hurt."

Kelsey smiled appreciatively. "Thank you, Henry. I won't

let you down again. I swear it."

When he was untied, he fell in behind the others as they started back toward the big top.

Most of the campfires had died by the time the four shadows began to move slowly between the tents and wagons. No celebration of the successful evening performance. At least the show people had respect for the late ringmaster. Everyone had gone to bed for the evening, making Raider's entrance much easier. Augie slipped away and headed back to his wagon as Masters had ordered.

As Raider ascended the steps of Ramona Masters's box wagon, he wondered if he had it in him to shoot a woman—even if she had the drop on him. Lights still burned in the nest of the Georgia Nightingale. She was awake, probably counting her money.

Raider knocked. No response. He knocked harder. "Give it up, Ramona. We know what you done. It won't do you any good to hide."

No sounds at all from inside.

Raider used his boot to splinter the door. He stuck his Winchester into the wagon and shouted a warning. When he looked into the dimly lighted recess, his face went white.

"Gone!" he cried. "Ramona checked out. Kelsey, you look in the back of the wagon, just in case."

The gunfighter obeyed without hesitation. He came back shaking his head. No sign of the Georgia Nightingale.

Masters gestured to an open safe behind his desk. "She cleaned out the kitty. All of it, gone, including the receipts from both performances."

Raider spun toward the door. "Harmon!"

But the roustabout's wagon was deserted as well. They had fled immediately after the show. Raider had to hand it to the Georgia Nightingale, she was sharp. They had gotten out quickly, on horseback.

"I got to go after her," Raider said. "I reckon she'll be tryin' to hop a train. She got any kin?"

"In Georgia," Masters replied. "Least that's what she told me."

Kelsey nodded. "Told me the same thing."

Masters drew back to take a swing. "You shitbird!"

Raider caught his wrist. "Now look here, both of you boys is just gonna have to take your tonic and live it out till it stops botherin' you. Ain't that it?"

Masters sighed. "Yeah, I reckon that's it. But don't expect me to shake hands with Kelsey."

"I don't mind a bit," the old gunfighter replied. "And I want to help you find her, Raider. I want to go along."

"I'm comin' too," Masters replied.

Raider knew he could move faster on his own, but he figured it wouldn't do any good to argue. "You boys is welcome to come. But don't expect me to wait if you can't keep up."

"We'll keep up," Kelsey replied. "I want my guns."

"Get Augie to tell you where he hid them."

Kelsey eyed the big man. "Any notions where she might run?"

Raider looked toward town. "She's too smart to head back into Kansas City. My guess would be that since they're on horseback, they'll be headin' for the nearest rail or stage stop."

Kelsey pointed south. "She used to talk about catchin' the stage for home. Said somethin' about Fire Creek bein' the best place."

"Plenty west of here, too," Raider replied. "And Ramona don't usually do what she says. But the trail will be warm when we find it. They ain't got but a couple of hours on us."

Kelsey started toward Augie's tent. The little man had gone back there to take off his clown makeup. Raider watched as the old gunfighter strode through the shadows.

Masters spat in Kelsey's direction. "How could he? How could he cuckold me like an old—"

"Like an old man?" Raider said. "You looked in the mirror lately?"

Masters balled up his fists. "She made a fool of me. She ran me around her little finger and then threw everything back in my face."

Raider tried to be consoling. "Best not to take that kind of stuff to heart, Henry. I mean, you did git what you went after. Probably got it good too, from the way things have fallen."

Masters was redfaced. "What do you know?"

The big man half smiled. "I know this: if you worry too much about women and the things they do, you won't have time for much else."

"I want to find that bitch," Masters growled. "I want to find her and . . . I want to get her."

Raider started out into the night. "Come on, Henry. Let's go see if we can find us some fast horses."

Masters followed the Pinkerton, inspiring wide-eyed stares from those few people still awake. "I'll explain it to them later," he said. "Have you got any idea which direction we're going in?"

"West," Raider replied.

It seemed like the natural direction for the Georgia Nightingale.

CHAPTER FOURTEEN

"There's the railroad station."

Raider sat on the back of a steady gray, peering to the southwest. Masters and Kelsey shifted on their mounts. They had been riding all night, into the morning. Kelsey seemed okay, but Masters obviously was not used to the rigors of the saddle.

The circus promoter wiped his forehead, peering toward the train stop. "Can you see her, Raider? Your eyes are better than mine."

Raider shook his head. "Come on. If she boarded the train here, the rail man ain't likely to have forgot about her."

They pounded the dry turf toward the tiny outpost. It was a lone station for cowboys and ranchers who were trying the newfangled prospect of rail-shipping their herds to market. The rail office manager was startled to see a trio of strangers so early in the day.

Raider quickly gave him a description of Bull Harmon and Ramona Masters. The rail man told them he had seen the man and the woman, but they had ridden on, westward, after he informed them that the train would not be arriving for another three days.

After he thanked the rail man, Raider swung back into the saddle.

Masters looked up, seemingly disheartened. "Ain't we even gonna rest?"

"Nope," was Raider's only reply.

Kelsey jumped onto his horse. "Stay back if you want, Henry. I'll keep Raider covered if he needs it."

Masters shook his head. "In for a dollar, in for a dime." He climbed onto his mount.

Their horses galloped for the hot, dusty horizon. Raider was in a hurry. He wanted to reach Ramona Masters before she harmed someone else. He knew better than to underestimate an opponent like Mrs. Masters, but he still wondered if he might slip a little if he was forced to draw down on a woman. And that might be all the edge the Georgia Nightingale would need.

Raider listed in the saddle, keeping his eyes peeled from side to side. Kelsey and Masters rode behind him, both of them reeling from the sun and the exhaustion. A man and a woman—Harmon and Ramona Masters—had ridden through Winslow Junction two days before. They just kept missing them, sometimes by hours.

The trail had not been an easy one to follow. Ramona and Harmon, both of them, knew how to zigzag, divert in another direction for a day or two and then resume the original route to the southwest. An old but effective trick, even when you knew they were doing it. Raider's superior tracking skills had come into play, but he still had to remain on his toes.

Behind him, he heard Kelsey wheezing. "I don't think they came this way, Arkansas. Ain't nothin' out here noways."

Masters agreed. "Maybe we ought to stop."

Raider shook his head. "I feel the sun on the back of my neck too. But I ain't stoppin'. Y'all lay back if you want."

Cougar eased his mount up next to Raider's. "Big man, anythin' I said about you Pinkertons, I take it back double."

Raider nodded, looking sideways at the old man.

"What's on your mind, boy?" Kelsey asked.

Raider smiled sheepishly. "I figure you've seen a lot in your time, Cougar. An old buzzard like you. I was just wonderin' somethin'."

Kelsey tipped back his sweat-stained Stetson. "Go on, ask me."

Raider laughed. "All right. Did you really kill a cougar with your bare hands?"

"I thought you was gonna ask me about Wade Turner." Kelsey replied.

"Naw, I figured that was your business."

Kelsey smiled halfheartedly. "Yes, I killed Wade Turner. No, I never killed a cougar with my bare hands." A pause. "I killed it with a knife."

Raider whistled. "You musta been one tough prospector."

Kelsey's smile vanished. "I still am, boy. I still am."

The big man turned back to look at Masters. The circus promoter was ash white, his lips were dry and cracked. But the old bulldog kept on riding.

"He's determined," Kelsey said.

Raider just nodded. He knew what Masters wanted. To look his young wife in the eye, to see how she felt when she saw him alive. Raider had the same feeling inside himself.

"Where you figure we are?" Kelsey asked.

Raider glanced out over the plain. "Somewhere in Oklahoma. If we're where I think we are, I want to cut south a few miles up."

"Why?"

"You'll see," Raider replied.

Kelsey had a dubious gleam in his gray eyes. "I think we mighta lost 'em, big man."

Raider shrugged. "Maybe. But anytime you feel like goin' your own way, you just rein right or left."

"I'll stay with you," Kelsey said.

"Why's that, Cougar?"

Kelsey leveled his eyes on the horizon. "Because the way I figure it, you're the best chance we got of findin' her."

Raider spurred his mount into the sun, with Kelsey and Masters following in his tracks.

They stood on a hot, windy rise, gazing down at a two-story house in the notch of a small natural basin. Kelsey and Masters peered at the same structure.

Raider pointed into the distance. "Annie," he said. "Annie Buttons. Runs a boardinghouse, or at least that's the nice name for it. People come in and out. Annie calls the girls her daughters. Only they ain't, if you get my drift. Masters, you hang back. Cougar and I'll go in."

Masters did not protest.

Raider started for his mount.

"You make this place sound dangerous," Kelsey said.

"It can be," the big man called from the saddle. "I'm goin' in the front door. You ought to cover the flank, maybe come in through the kitchen."

Kelsey agreed that would be best.

They galloped down into the basin, making for the house.

Raider tied his horse on the hitching post out front. Kelsey went around to the back door. You could never be sure who might be sleeping at Annie's, Raider thought. Sometimes her customers would draw down on you if you even looked like a lawman—or a law-abiding citizen, for that matter.

Raider took a deep breath and started up the steps. He didn't bother to knock. When he entered the dim enclosure, he heard plates rattling at the dinner table. A dirty-haired woman came out to greet him.

"Remember me, Annie?"

She did not remember him. "You're too late for dinner. It's all gone."

Raider shook his head. "I ain't here for dinner. I'm looking for a couple of—"

"This hombre botherin' you, Annie?"

Her dinner guests had risen from the table to come into the parlor. Four tall, rough men in gray dusters stood behind her. Raider's hand hung slack by his Colt. He did not want to shoot it out with them.

"Howdy," the big man said. "Ain't no need for anybody to miss their dinner. I'm just wantin' to—"

"Clear out," said one of the duster men.

Raider eyed him, staring until he looked away. "I need to ask Annie a few questions," he said. "Ain't much more to it than that."

One of the duster men said, "He's a lawman."

"It ain't like that," Raider insisted.

Annie fidgeted in front of her houseguests. "Maybe you ought to go, stranger. This ain't a good time."

"Time is real important, ma'am," Raider replied. "You

see, I'm lookin' for this woman and this man. They stole somethin'—"

"I told you he was the law!"

Raider exhaled. "I ain't got no business with you, pardner."

Annie moved away, back into the dining room.

The big man from Arkansas was looking at four guns as they drew back their coats.

"Give him the chance to draw first," said the front man.

"Four to one," Raider muttered. "All right, boys, let's do it."

He went for his Colt.

Two of them were fast. Raider beat both of them to the punch. He fired twice, but to his surprise, all four of them fell.

Raider looked back into the dining room to see Cougar Jake Kelsey holding two smoking Colts. The four drifters had not even gotten off a shot.

"Thanks, Jake, I . . . hey . . . don't . . ."

Cougar Jake seemed to be pointing his open-bore Colt at the big man's head. Raider hit the floor, rolling, coming up with his Peacemaker. Kelsey fired twice where Raider had been standing. A man with a shotgun staggered forward, two holes in his chest. He smashed face-first into the floor.

Raider gaped at the dead man who had almost put a hole in his back. "I reckon I owe you for that one, Jake. You saved my damn life."

Kelsey kept his Colts drawn, anticipating an attack from another direction.

Annie stuck her head back into the parlor. "That's all of them. Five. Only other people is them two upstairs."

Raider's eyes opened wider. He described Ramona and Harmon. Annie nodded. That was them. They had been there for two days and had never come out of the room.

Raider nodded at Kelsey. "With all the shootin', they know we're here."

"Let's get her."

They started slowly up the stairs, listening for signs of movement. Nothing but quiet. Ramona and her boyfriend were laying low. Probably armed to the teeth.

"Ramona!" Raider called. "Bull Harmon! You can't get

through us. Me and Cougar Jake are down here."

Raider kept waiting to hear the sliding of a second-story window. Still no sound except the creaking of the stairs. They went up a few more steps. Raider had his Peacemaker in front of him, ready to squeeze off a couple of rounds.

"Harmon!"

They stepped onto the second floor.

Raider gestured with the barrel of his weapon. "Check the bathroom. I'll start with this first door."

Kelsey moved slowly down the corridor.

One by one, Raider threw open the room doors. Nothing but empty beds. He saw Kelsey coming out of the bathroom, shaking his head.

Raider moved toward the last room. "They got to be in here."

The door was locked.

Raider splintered the jamb with one kick. He lowered the Colt at the man who was lying in bed. "Don't move, Harmon."

Harmon did not stir.

"Where's Ramona?" Kelsey said.

"Ask him." Raider nodded toward Harmon.

Kelsey reached over to pull the covers away from Harmon . . . His skin was death blue. Throat cut from ear to ear, thick blood sticky on the sheets. He was cold stone dead.

Kelsey put the covers over the body of the former roustabout. "She got him. The Georgia Nightingale. She's more like a damned Arizona vulture."

"Didn't need him anymore," Raider rejoined. "What a sucker."

"Easy. I was her sucker too."

Raider nodded. "Come on. Let's go talk to Annie."

"Maybe Ramona's still in the house," Kelsey offered.

"No. Annie said they ain't been down for two days. My guess is that she killed him the first night and then bolted when nobody was awake."

"The attic?"

Raider shrugged. "Check if you like."

The big Pinkerton went back downstairs to question the landlady of the borderland sleeping house. Annie was cooperative, but only after extracting the promise that Raider and Kelsey would bury the bodies. Raider had finished talking to her by the time Kelsey came down from the attic.

"She ain't there," the old gunfighter said.

"I know," Raider replied. "She's gone to catch the stage."

Kelsey shot Raider a doubtful glance. "How you know that?"

"She was askin' Annie about stage and train. Ain't no train hereabouts. Has to be the stage."

Kelsey started for the door. "Let's get movin'."

Raider stopped him. "Hold up. We got a little chore to do."

"Chore?"

The big man gestured toward the bodies. "We got to plant these fine citizens before we go. Annie doesn't want 'em lyin' around."

Kelsey bristled. "She's gone. She's gettin' away. If we stay here, we might lose her."

"I got to keep my promise to Annie," Raider replied. "I said I'd bury 'em and I will. If I back out, she'll tell me about it when I'm back this way again."

Kelsey slammed his fist into his hand. "Damn it all, she's as smart as the devil's mistress."

Raider gestured toward the rise where Masters waited for them. "Better go up and tell Henry to get down here. He'll be wonderin' what all the shootin' was about."

Kelsey nodded. "Where next?"

Raider peered away from the sun. "Back east."

"Why east?"

"Elmira," Raider replied. "Nearest stage stop. She's led us along for a while. Now she'll be wantin' to get back to her kin."

The World's Oldest Living Gunfighter nodded. "Makes sense. You been right so far."

Raider turned back to their hostess, Annie, who was going through the pockets of the dead men. "You got a shovel around here, Annie."

"In the shed," she replied without looking up.

"We all dig," Raider said to Kelsey. "Be sure you tell that to Masters."

Kelsey nodded, heading back up the rise.

Raider started for the shed. He didn't mind digging one big grave for all five of them. Six if you threw in the late Bull Harmon. He had to give it to Ramona—she was rolling along in fine fashion. And the big man had to admit to himself that he was thoroughly enjoying the chase.

CHAPTER FIFTEEN

All afternoon, Raider, Kelsey, and Masters had been making for the crest of a high ridge to the southwest. They were somewhere in Oklahoma, still a day behind Ramona Masters. She had turned back east, but then she had caught a stage west again, a line that ended in Chicopee, near the Texas border. With fresh horses, they would have been able to catch her in no time, but the mounts taken from the circus remuda were almost worn out.

"We'll rest 'em when we reach that rise," Raider said. "Should be some shade there."

Masters was sweating bullets. "Is it my imagination or is that ridge moving further away with each step we take?"

"Just a mirage," Raider said. "Keep movin'."

Kelsey wiped his forehead with the back of his hand. "I hope there's some water there. This heat is killin' me."

The sun had fallen behind the ridge by the time they were able to look up at the unusual rock formations. There was water, a slow trickle from above. They filled their canteens and then watered the horses.

Raider suggested they get moving, to find a place to camp before it got dark.

"What's wrong with this place?" Masters asked.

The circus promoter clearly did not want to ride anymore.

But Raider kept looking above them, his eyes darting back and forth between the afternoon shadows. "No, Henry. We'd better go."

Kelsey nodded. "I been seein' 'em too. What tribe, big man?"

Raider shrugged. "Cherokee, maybe. Although I don't know what they'd be doin' this far south."

Masters face turned white. "Indians?"

"Nothin' to worry about," Raider replied. "If we clear out, they'll just let us be. Probably a huntin' party with special permission to leave the reservation. If we . . . Henry, don't!"

Masters had reached for the Winchester on the side of Raider's saddle. As soon as his hand hit the rifle butt, an arrow thudded into the stock wood between his fingers. The circus promoter drew back his hand.

Raider looked at the arrow. "Yep. Cherokee, all right. Don't make no more sudden movements, Henry."

Masters's fingers were trembling. "But they tried to kill me."

"No," Raider said. "They just warned you. If they had wanted you dead, that arrow would be stickin' out of your heart."

Masters clutched his chest, which was still sore from the blank wounds.

Kelsey's hands hung near his twin six-shooters. "I oughta give 'em a taste of my special loads."

Raider kept his black eyes turned upward. If the Indians wanted something they'd come down. They'd let him know.

"Here he comes," the big man said, pointing to the small figure that slipped between the rocks.

A short, brightly garbed Cherokee brave came toward them from the base of the ridge. He smiled up at Raider, grabbing the reins of all three horses. When Raider tried to take back the reins, he heard rifle levers above him.

"They got guns too."

Another brave came behind the first emissary to take their weapons.

"Y'all savvy any English?" Raider asked.

The first man nodded. "You come with us."

"How far are you from the reservation?" Kelsey asked. "I

mean, you ain't even supposed to be down this way."

The brave smiled. "New treaty. We hunt here. You come with us."

He started to lead the horses toward a pass in the ridge. There was nothing for them to do but follow. Kelsey and Masters stayed behind Raider, coming in his tracks.

"Raider," Masters asked, "where are they takin' us?"

"To their camp," the big man replied.

"Why?"

"Because they can," Kelsey offered.

Raider shook his head. "I don't think they'll kill us. Let's just do what they say. The place we're headin' for ain't far from here. They've got to let us go sooner or later."

Masters looked frightened now. "I hope so."

As they traversed the rock-strewn trail, a welcoming committee of armed braves followed along the ridge above them. Raider wondered at the colorful outfits worn by the braves. Bright gingham and cotton had been used for their tunics and pants. They were not western Indians, but transported from the East by Old Hickory's removal plan. They weren't hostile, but sometimes the Cherokee could get their backs up.

When they cleared the pass, the sentry braves went back to their spots on the ridge. Another band of armed men greeted the visitors. They were wearing boots and felt hats. The Cherokee had taken quickly to the ways of the white man. As they made for the smoking fire in the middle of the hunting party encampment, Raider wondered if the Cherokee had any mercy left for the white man.

Four makeshift dwellings were set up in a square configuration, with a fifth one resting in the middle of the box. Raider figured the party to be about fifteen to twenty braves. The tent in the middle belonged to the leader. Best to call him out and get it over with.

"Who's your chief?" Raider asked one of the braves.

"Storm Walker," came the reply.

"Storm Walker!" Raider cried. "Get on out here."

An angry face appeared from the opening of the tepee. He was big. And ugly. Scars across his face attested to the knife fights he had been in. There was a bullet scar in his chest.

When Storm Walker spoke, his English was clear and precise. "You have disturbed me, white man."

Raider grimaced, squinting at the Cherokee chief. "I ain't too happy about your men takin' us prisoner."

Storm Walker thumped his bare chest. "I go where I want. My father was Thunder Chief. We do not listen to the white man."

Raider shook his head. "Storm Walker, you sure are stretchin' your territory. I mean, you can probably get away with huntin' along the borderland if the Indian agent don't find you, but if you cause any trouble, the militia is gonna be ridin' down on you."

Storm Walker paced back and forth, eyeing the three of them. "I don't fear the militia. I am as educated as the blue-coated soldiers. I went to school in the East."

Raider nodded. "That's good, Storm Walker. Then maybe you'll be smart enough to let us go."

Storm Walked focused on Raider's black eyes. "Who are you? What are your names? Why are you here?"

Raider pointed to Masters. "That little feller is a great showman. He puts on what you call a circus. Now a circus is—"

"I know what a circus is," Storm Walker cried. "Who is the old man?"

"A great warrior," Raider replied. "His name is Cougar Kelsey. He can shoot as good as any man alive."

Storm Walker scoffed. "He cannot shoot better than I!"

Raider's eyes glistened. He saw the opening. "Maybe we should smoke on it, Storm Walker. Unless you got somethin' against smokin' the peace pipe with a couple of white men."

Storm Walker glared at him. "We smoke."

He went back inside the tepee.

Masters leaned in toward Raider. "What are you goin' to do?"

"Just be still," the big man replied. "Kelsey, you come with me."

Cougar Jake was half smiling. "What're you up to, Arkansas?"

"Just play along. And if he hands you the pipe, don't take in none of the smoke. It might fog your head."

With that, the two tall man strode into Storm Walker's tepee.

* * *

"Confound it, Allan, have you seen these reports?" Wagner held up a letter from the police chief of Kansas City.

Pinkerton nodded. "I've seen it. It says that Raider left Kansas City two weeks ago, searching for some woman. No one has heard from him since then."

"That's not all," Wagner railed. "There's some doubt as to whether Henry Masters is alive or dead."

Pinkerton exhaled. "I know. I read it, Wagner."

Raider's immediate supervisor turned his eyes up to the map. "Where could he be?" Wagner dropped the report on Pinkerton's desk.

Pinkerton lifted the report, but he did not read it again. "Raider has his own way of doing things, Wagner. You know that. We just have to trust him until we find out what he's really up to."

Wagner moved to the window, looking out. "I say we call him in. Send someone after him to bring him back."

"No."

"But it makes sense to—"

Pinkerton waved him off. "It wouldn't do any good. Raider will turn up when he's ready."

"Or when he's dead," Wagner rejoined.

"Send a wire to the Texas Rangers if it will make you feel better," Pinkerton offered. "Ask them to look out for Raider."

Wagner left the room without a word.

Pinkerton couldn't blame him for being nervous. Raider was almost uncontrollable now that Doc Weatherbee was no longer with him. Had it been a mistake to assign him to the circus job?

An hour later, Wagner came back into the room. He had sent the wire to Texas. As far as the rangers knew, Raider was nowhere near the Lone Star state. They hadn't seen hide nor hair of him.

Storm Walker drew on the pipe and handed it to Raider. The big man pretended to smoke a substance that wasn't even close to being tobacco. He gave the pipe to Kelsey, who also feigned inhalation of the strong smoke.

"You have not told me why you have come here," Storm Walker demanded.

Raider gestured with his hands. "We've come a long way, searching for a woman. She has hurt many people. She has stolen gold and has been unfaithful to her husband. We must catch her before she hurts more people."

Storm Walker uncrossed his legs and stood up. "Men who are tricked by women are foolish."

Raider nodded. "You ain't gonna get no argument from me, Storm Walker. But it happens. You tellin' me a filly ain't never got your goat?"

Storm Walker's brow fretted. "I don't have a goat."

Kelsey looked up at the big brave. "You got to let us go, Chief. We got to catch up to Ramona. If she don't—"

"Silence!" Storm Walker reached for the pipe, which was lying next to the fire. "Smoke."

They passed the pipe again. Storm Walker's eyes were red-streaked. He swayed a little, and his face slacked into a dull grin.

Raider decided it was time to push him. "Storm Walker. I heard your name before. Your father was a great chief."

Storm Walker balled up his fist and waved it in the air. "I am greater. I can ride, hunt, shoot, and fight better than any white man."

Raider gestured to his friend Kelsey. "This man is a great mountain lion. He is called Cougar. Of all my people, he is the best at shooting a gun. He can hit birds on the wing with his pistol."

"Ha!" Storm Walker scoffed. "I am better."

Raider wondered if he might be nailing shut their coffins. But he kept on. "You are not better than Cougar. And you are not better than me. I am the greatest fighter. Much better than you. And if you say you are better, then you must prove it."

Storm Walker crossed his arms. "I will not."

Raider rose from the ground. "Then I must ride back to the reservation and tell Thunder Chief that his son is afraid to test himself against the guns and fists of the white man."

As Raider turned away, he heard the lever of a Winchester. He looked back to see Storm Walker staring down the barrel at him.

Raider didn't move. "You gonna shoot me?" he asked.

Storm Walker lowered the barrel. "I am better."

Raider smiled. "Shootin' or fightin'. Which one will it be?"

The Cherokee chief lifted his rifle. "Shoot!"

"And if Kelsey is better, then you let us go?"

Storm Walker smiled. "What if I am better?"

Raider shrugged. "You tell me."

Storm Walker only laughed and directed them outside.

Masters greeted them with a bellowing cry of despair. The circus promoter had been tied to a pole, his wrists bound so that his arms were above his head. And to top the injury with a helping of insult, Masters had been forced to don a ragged calico dress!

"I'll be . . ." Kelsey started.

Raider shook his head. "Crazy Injuns."

"Get me out of this," Masters cried.

Kelsey squinted at his partner. "You think they'll kill him?"

Raider sighed. "I don't know. I doubt it. Looks like they just want to mess with us. I'm countin' on you to use them special loads to mess right back."

Storm Walker strode forward with Kelsey's guns in hand. He gave them to the World's Oldest Living Gunfighter, who immediately checked his shells. Kelsey's face went white.

"What is it?" Raider asked.

"He's loaded my guns with slugs from your Colts," Kelsey replied. "I got to shoot with regular cartridges."

Storm Walker smiled. "Ready?"

Kelsey had no choice but to nod.

"You can do it," Raider urged. "Just shoot straight. You got a good hand and a good pair of eyes."

"Raider, I don't know if I can."

Raider gestured toward the trussed-up Masters. "You better do it, pardner, otherwise we'll all be wearin' dresses."

Kelsey shook his head in disgust. "Is that some kinda Injun nonsense?"

"Naw," Raider replied. "I seen it in white men too."

Storm Walker had determined that the targets for the shooting match would be small round vessels of dried clay. He set up four targets and walked back to where Raider and Kelsey were standing. Immediately, Storm Walker raised his rifle and fired off four shots that sent three of the targets flying into nothing. The fourth one just shattered into two halves.

Storm Walker gestured toward the targets. "See? I am better."

Raider nodded. "Not bad. Kelsey, you ready?"

Cougar Jake had sweat pouring down his face. He indicated that he was prepared to shoot. He pointed upward. He wanted Raider to toss the targets into the air.

Could he hit them without his special loads?

Raider walked out to the same distance and picked up four of the dried clay vessels. But instead of setting them on the ground, he threw all four of them skyward. The big man held his breath.

Kelsey drew down, his pistols exploding.

The targets shattered against the evening sky, bursting into a thousand pieces in the last rays of red sun.

Raider whooped a Rebel war cry.

Kelsey grinned and dropped the pistols back into his holsters. "I reckon I still got it."

Storm Walker frowned in disbelief. "No. It can't be!"

"Believe it, Chief," Raider replied. "You got to let us go."

But Storm Walker was not ready to give up. He had his own man throw four balls into the air. He could not hit one of them with his rifle. He kept on trying until the sun was completely gone. Finally he threw his rifle to the ground, seething with anger and hatred.

Raider started for Masters. "I'll just be untyin' this gentleman so we can get the hell out of here."

Cherokee braves moved to stop him with their rifles.

Storm Walker cried out.

For a terrifying instant, everyone was frozen silent.

Raider glared at the scarred face. "You must keep your word. Cougar has proved he's better. You must let us go."

"No!" Storm Walker cried. "You all stay."

Kelsey's hands fell toward his twin Peacemakers.

Raider stopped him from drawing, stepping between the old shootist and the irate chief. "If you don't let us go, I will tell your people that you broke your word. That you acted like a coward."

Storm Walker raised his fist. "How many times has the

white man broken his word to the Cherokee?"

Raider nodded. "I can't argue with that. But one thing I want to say, Storm Walker. Do you want to be like the white man?"

Storm Walker sat down on the ground, crossing his legs, flopping defeatedly on his backside. "Let them go," he muttered. "Give them their guns and their horses and turn them loose."

Raider cut Masters free and the three of them wasted no time mounting their horses.

Masters looked down at the calico dress. "I want to change back into my suit, Raider!"

Raider turned his mount west. "You can put it on later. But we best be clearin' out of here while these boys is actin' like good sports."

When they had ridden a half mile, the sound of whooping Cherokees rose up behind them. Storm Walker and his braves gave chase for another couple of miles before they decided to quit. They really didn't want to catch them, just make a little noise.

Finally they outran the Cherokees, slowing in the darkness.

"Savages," Masters grumbled. "I hate them."

Raider squinted at the circus promoter. "They hate you too, Henry. We better stop so you can put on your suit." The big man refrained from obvious jokes about the calico dress.

Kelsey stared out into the darkness of the plain. "We gonna make camp?"

Raider shrugged. "I'd just as soon keep ridin'. I'm too bunched up to sleep. My blood's goin'."

Masters, who was pulling on his pants, sighed. "I would like some rest. I feel like I've been beaten with a stick."

But when Raider reminded the showman that they were close to catching up with his young wife, Masters was ready to ride again.

CHAPTER SIXTEEN

Raider pointed into the shallow hollow where the small town sat without a single sign of motion. "Chicopee," he said. "Don't look like much."

Kelsey rubbed a pain in his back. "And we rode all night to get here."

"No attendant at the stage depot," Raider said. "Train depot quiet. That's why she wanted to come here. The train will take her back east."

Masters grunted. "Is Ramona down there?"

"I don't see her," the big man replied. "I don't see nobody."

Kelsey squinted at the stage depot. "I wonder if the coach has come in yet?"

Raider urged his mount down the narrow trail. "Ain't but one way to find out. Spread wide and keep it slow." He tossed the rifle back to Masters. "Don't freeze if we get shot at, Henry. If we're ambushed, follow my lead."

They descended toward the sleepy early-morning town.

Chicopee was small—a general store, a few abandoned structures, a livery that had gone out of business, one dirt street, and a stray dog. The cattle pens and the railroad were the only indication that anyone even cared about the grimy hamlet. Nobody seemed to notice their entrance.

Kelsey shook his head. "Why would she run to a place like this?"

"Because," Raider replied, his eyes darting from side to side, "it's the most out-in-the-boondocks place where she could double back. She's come in a circle. Probably hopin' to get back to Oklahoma City, make the jump to a train that would take her south to New Orleans or Atlanta. She's slick, men. Don't underestimate her."

Of course, neither of the two wronged lovers would make that mistake.

Kelsey stiffened a little. "She coulda got off that stage anytime."

"Maybe," Raider said. "But she bought a ticket all the way to Chicopee. And the train station is here too."

But there was no trainman on duty. No one at the stage stop either. They headed for the general store. A man with a sheriff's badge met them on the porch. He was holding a double-barreled shotgun.

"You boys come lookin' for trouble?"

He was a young man with a fuzzy beard. Fire in his blue eyes. The only law in Chicopee, Raider thought. Probably self-appointed.

Raider tipped his hat. "Just lookin' for the stage man. Or the trainman. Know if they're hereabouts?"

"I'm them," the young man replied. "What you wantin'?"

"We're lookin' for a woman." Raider pointed back to the stage stop. "She woulda come in on the stage, probably to wait for the train."

The man's eye lifted from the bead of the shotgun.

Kelsey described Ramona—the dark hair, ample breasts, the sultry nature of her character.

"She killed a man," Masters added. "Maybe a few more that we don't know about."

A tension had lodged in the man's face. He wasn't a bad-looking kid. Just the kind who might be weak enough. His blue eyes looked down the barrel of the gun again.

"Ain't seen no woman like that."

His mouth was dry. Raider could see the lather on his lips. Sweat pouring down his face.

Kelsey's hand dropped slowly toward his right holster.

"Now see here, kid. I was plantin' men when you were still on your momma's knee. Now you better tell us if—"

Raider threw out his hand. "No, Cougar. This boy seems like an honest man. If Ramona had been through here, he would tell us. Wouldn't you, boy?"

The man hesitated before he nodded cautiously. "Yeah, that's right. If she had been here, I woulda told you. Now you boys clear out."

Masters snarled at the Chicopee sheriff, "We'd like to rest and have a hot meal at least."

The sheriff waved the barrel of the scattergun. "There's a cornfield just over that rise. Pick all you want. Shoot a rabbit if you care to, but just keep goin' after you et. I don't want no strangers around here."

"We're on our way," Raider replied, smiling. "Just one thing. When's that train due in?"

The sheriff shrugged. "Day after tomorrow. Only makes one trip a month. Three when the cattle come in."

The big man from Arkansas tipped his hat. "Much obliged, Sheriff. We won't trouble you no more."

He turned his mount and started out of town.

Kelsey and Masters rode up next to him.

"Are you crazy?" Kelsey said. "That boy was hidin' somethin'."

Masters scowled at the big man. "We have to rest. We lost her trail. We just have to admit it to ourselves."

Raider kept on going. "Wait, boys, until we get out of town. Then we can pick some corn and double back here. That livery should be a good place to hide."

Kelsey's eyes narrowed. "What you got in mind?"

Raider pulled down his Stetson to block the hot sun. "We'll watch. Then we find out if that sheriff is lyin'."

Masters suddenly nodded. "I see what you mean. He looks just like the kind Ramona could wrap around her finger."

Kelsey shook his head. "She ain't here, I'm tellin' you."

"Well, Cougar," Raider replied, "you don't have to stay with us."

"Then I'm leavin'," Kelsey said. He gazed to the south. "I'm goin' back that way. I just got a hunch that she's at one of those other stage stops. I've got to go try my own luck."

Raider reined back. "Kelsey, don't ruin it if you find her.

You just take her into custody and lock her up in the nearest hoosegow. Then you come and get me. Understood?"

"I'll bring her right back to Kansas City," Kelsey said. "You can find me there if you don't hear from me again."

The World's Oldest Living Gunfighter spurred his mount to the south. Raider watched until he was out of sight. Cougar had gotten awfully headstrong in a hurry. Raider didn't rightly know how to read that.

Masters squinted toward the horizon. "Didn't even say goodbye to me."

"You figured he would?" Raider asked.

Masters laughed cynically. "No, I don't reckon he would."

"Come on, Henry, let's go pick some corn."

Raider and Masters took to the loft in the old abandoned livery. From there they were able to observe the scant comings and goings around Chicopee. There wasn't much action, with the exception of the stray dog and his territorial markings.

Toward the afternoon, Masters started talking to himself. "I'll kill her. That's what I'll do. Shoot her. It's the only way I can get her to respect me."

Raider eyed the circus promoter. "Don't go loco on me, Henry. I'm gonna need you later. If I'm right."

"Right about what?" Henry asked.

Raider opened the loft door slightly and pointed out. "Right about that."

Masters peered out into the street. Strolling down the muddy avenue for an afternoon walk were the sheriff and a young woman. She had dark hair and the face of an angel. When they heard her laughter, it was like the song of the nightingale. The Georgia Nightingale.

Masters opened his mouth to shout her name. Raider caught him, smothering the words with the palm of his hand. He wrestled Masters to the floor and pinned him until he was motionless.

"I was right, Henry," the big man whispered. "She's doin' her spell on the sheriff there. Got him steppin'. Only we want her to think she's free. That way we can trick her into tellin' us everything. I got the plan if you're willin' to go along with it."

Masters nodded, prompting Raider to lift his hand away.

"Why don't you go down there and arrest her?" he pleaded.

"Evidence," Raider replied. "Right now, what do we have? She left you when she thought you were dead and took money that was rightfully hers. Otherwise we can't link her to anybody's killin'. She's gonna hang, Henry, if I have anythin' to say about it."

Masters looked at the big man. "You mean she may be executed?"

Raider nodded. "If we can nail her on the killin'."

Masters got up, staring out of a crack in the door. "Ramona, hanged. I don't know."

Her laughter rose in the afternoon quiet.

"How can she be so happy?" Masters growled. "How can she laugh after she killed Bull Harmon?"

"We wait and watch," Raider said. "And then we move when the time is right. No slip-ups this time."

Raider watched as Masters steamed. He wondered if the circus promoter would ask to pull the handle on the gallows when they strung up his wife. Raider was glad the man had anger in his eyes. Raider wanted him ready for the final act. And the way he figured, Masters was just the showman to pull it off.

CHAPTER SEVENTEEN

Two days later, at nine o'clock in the morning, the train chugged into Chicopee. Ramona Masters sashayed down the dirt street with the young sheriff carrying her baggage. After the trunks were loaded onto the railcar, Ramona lingered on the platform, lavishing the blue-eyed man with long kisses.

Raider watched from the rail office window. Masters stood behind him, ready to move. The big man had shown his Pinkerton credentials to the engineer and the conductor of the train. After he had explained the situation, they had agreed to cooperate with his plan.

Masters leaned past the Pinkerton detective. "What's she doin'?"

"Sayin' goodbye," Raider replied. "Here comes the conductor. He's makin' her board."

Masters leaned farther out the window. "Look at her. She's laughing with the conductor now. That teasin' little . . . Oh, no!" He dropped back suddenly.

"What happened, Henry?"

Masters gritted his teeth. "She saw me. She saw my face."

Raider smiled. "Good. Real good."

"No," Masters replied. "She saw me, I'm tellin' you. She grimaced for a moment."

173

Raider tipped back his Stetson. "It couldn't have worked out better. A look at your mug in the window. Yep, we're off on the right track."

The train whistle screeched.

Raider eased toward the door. "Time to go."

Masters held up his trembling hands. "Look at me. I've been in a center ring a thousand times, but now I'm as nervous as a first-timer on opening night."

A knock at the door. "She's on the train," the conductor said.

Raider nodded to Masters. "All set. Let's take up in the mail car where she can't see us."

The big man picked up his Winchester, which was leaning against the wall.

Masters shot him a cautious glance. "Please, don't shoot her."

"I won't," the tall Pinkerton replied. "Unless she tries to shoot me. Then . . ."

"All right, all right."

"Remember, Henry, just like we rehearsed it in the barn."

Masters nodded. It was a good plan, not like the scheme that had missed in Kansas City. They had been up all night, ironing out the particulars, setting up the props. All they had to do was wait for the sun to go down. Then they would trap her.

When the train whistle blew again, they ran quickly for the huge door, climbing into the mail car to wait for night.

The train chugged eastward, stopping every so often to pick up the few passengers scattered along the route. The largest group of travelers would board in Oklahoma City, the first real city on the line. So it was no problem for the conductor to keep Ramona Masters isolated in the front passenger car, shuffling the rest of the riders to the second car. Some of the people complained, but the conductor assured them that they did not want to sit close to the engine, where sparks and cinders flew from the belching smokestack.

If Ramona Masters suspected any of the preparations that were being made in her dubious honor, she did not show it. She simply leaned back and smirked at the passing landscape, no doubt feeling richer than she had before she left Kansas

City. The Georgia Nightingale figured she was home free, sitting in the catbird seat.

She called for the conductor as he strode between the seats.

He tried not to show his nervousness. "Yes, miss?"

She touched his hand. "I want to thank you for keeping this car free of those undesirable types. Here, for you."

She tried to put a gold coin in his palm.

The conductor drew back, sweat pouring off his brow. "I'm sorry, miss. I'm not allowed to accept gratuities."

She laughed. "Oh? Well, thank you just the same."

The conductor tipped his hat and started walking again. Ramona did not see him slip through the rear door of the car. Nor was she aware that he locked the door from the outside, just as Raider had told him to do.

Her eyes turned lazily to the purple shadows of the plain. Dusk had begun to settle in. Ramona watched until the plain was completely dark. Then the Georgia Nightingale glanced up at the gas lamps on both sides of the car. Why weren't the lamps lit?

"Conductor?"

But he was no longer there.

Ramona Masters stood up and felt her way through the shadows to the back door. When she found it locked, she pounded hard but to no avail. Her cries for the conductor were not heeded.

When she turned away from the door, she froze, gripping the edge of the train seat. She had heard it. Or had she?

Ramona.

Someone had called her name in a weak voice. Or was it the noise of the train engine? It was so hard to tell in the dark. Why didn't the conductor light those lamps?

Ramona.

The drawn-out sound of her name had been unmistakable. "Who's there? Conductor? Who is it?"

A dim, yellowish light glowed at the other end of the car.

Ramona stepped forward. "Conductor?"

The figure moved toward her. A man, his face death-white. Ramona still did not recognize him.

"Who are you? What are you doing?" she demanded.

The man raised a crooked finger. "Have you forgotten me, Ramona?"

She moved closer, straining her eyes in the dim glow. "Who are you?"

Henry Masters was doing exactly as Raider had instructed him. They had even rigged a special candle that Masters wore on his belt. The flame was shielded from his wife's direct gaze by a tin plate, but the flickering fire cast a silvery reflection on Masters's flour-powdered face.

Masters came near enough for her to see his eyes. "I have come for you, Ramona. I have come to take you with me. You will be my wife for all eternity. My dead bride."

Her eyes swelled open and she teetered on weak legs. "Henry?" She almost swallowed his name.

"Yes. I am Henry. I have come to take you with me. It is time for you to die, Ramona."

She pinched herself. "I'm dreaming. I'm asleep, that's it."

Masters made his voice into a high-pitched chant. "No, my love. You must come with me. I am dead and you must be the same. You will be my queen in Hell."

"Hell?"

"God punishes the wicked, Ramona."

She leaned forward, her face desperate. "No, Henry. Please. Leave me alone. I never did anything to you."

Masters raised a crooked, indicting finger. "I am with the Lord of Darkness, Ramona. He deems that you have served him well. Satan wants you at his side."

She shook her head, her eyes glassy. "This can't be happening."

Masters gestured with his hand. "Come, we must go."

Her screams rose above the noise of the steam engine. "Conductor? Conductor? Someone, help me!"

Masters shook his head slowly. "No one can help you, Ramona. You are doomed to the fires of Hell for all eternity."

She dropped down on her knees. "Henry, I'm sorry. I never wanted to kill you. *He* made me do it."

His eyes flared wide. "Confess, woman. Confess your sins and you will know God's mercy."

The Georgia Nightingale was ready to take any way out. "Yes, I'm guilty. God forgive me. Please, don't take me, Henry!"

Masters kept his finger pointed at her. "Adulteress!"

She put her hands together, praying. "Yes. Forgive me."

"Thief!"

She shook her head. "No, I didn't mean to—"

"I know all, Ramona. You cannot lie to me!"

She lowered her head, tears streaming down her face. "Yes, I'm a thief. I confess it."

"You stole the gold in Lexington, from the Wells Fargo office!"

"Yes," she cried, her face in her hands. "But I wasn't alone. *He* helped me. And I did it for you, Henry. For the circus!"

"Murderess!"

"No! I swear it."

"You killed Ilana," he accused in his ghostly voice.

"No, it was Harmon. He was trying to shoot you. He wanted to marry me and take over the circus. I wouldn't have killed that girl, even if she *was* a bigger draw than me."

He leaned over her. "You killed Bull Harmon."

Her mouth quivered. "No, I—"

"Confess!"

"Yes, I cut his throat."

"And me, Ramona. You tried to kill me."

"No, Henry."

"You drugged me and then you dressed up like the professor. And then you shot me twice and ran through the camp so everyone would think Excalibur had shot me."

"Yes," she sobbed. "I'm so sorry, Henry. I never wanted to hurt you. I swear it. I . . . what . . . who's there?"

A brighter light came up in the car. Raider stood at the other end of the aisle holding the match he had used to torch one of the gas lamps. Ramona rose to her feet, glaring at the big man.

Raider strode down the aisle, his gun drawn. "I think we've heard enough, Henry. I'm the witness to her confession. I'll say so at the trial."

Ramona, who was growing angry, gaped at her husband, who was wiping the flour from his face. "You tricked me!" she screeched. "But how? How are you still alive?"

Masters scowled triumphantly. "When you dressed up as Excalibur, you chose the wrong weapon, Ramona. You used one of the blank guns from the mock Indian battle. Too bad you don't know much about firearms."

A hateful expression glazed over her countenance. "Yes," she replied coldly. "I should have been more thorough."

Raider moved in closer to keep her from attacking Henry Masters. "Let me ask you somethin', honey. How the hell did you get the professor to run mad through the camp?"

She laughed, dropping down into the train seat. "You mean you don't know? After everything else, you really haven't figured it out?"

Raider shrugged. "I s'pose Harmon helped you. I mean, you talked him into tryin' to kill Henry durin' a performance. But instead you killed my friend Ilana."

There were no more tears in Ramona's eyes. "That little bitch," she muttered. "I was glad he shot her. Strutting her ass all over the ring like she was the whole circus. I was happy after she got it. It was almost as good as killing Henry."

Masters shook his head in disgust. "But you didn't kill me, Ramona. I'm alive."

"Don't remind me," she replied.

Masters moved toward her with a piece of rope he had taken from his back pocket. "Better get her hands tied before she causes more trouble."

Raider stopped the circus man. "Not just yet. I have another question for her." He stared right through the icy beauty. "The Wells Fargo robbery in Lexington. How'd you pull that off?"

She cackled with mocking laughter. "How do you think? A man was in charge of the office. I used what God gave me. When his pants were down, my partner moved in and clobbered him."

Masters slammed his fist into his palm. "How could Bull Harmon be so disloyal to me after all these years?"

Ramona's eyes narrowed. "Harmon?"

Raider glared at her. "Wasn't Harmon workin' with you?"

"Only at the end." She smiled. "You really don't know, do you?"

The big man tipped back his Stetson. "Maybe I don't. Why don't you just tell us straight out?"

"It was Kelsey," she replied. "Harmon wanted me all along, but I kept him at distance until I needed him for a getaway. But Kelsey planned all of it. The Wells Fargo part,

Henry's murder. He even came up with the scheme to shoot Henry during the performance. I talked Harmon into pulling the trigger, but Kelsey was the mastermind."

Raider and Masters looked at each other.

"No wonder Kelsey took off," Masters said.

Ramona had a good laugh. "Big detective, huh. You couldn't see the truth if it was buzzing around your nose."

Raider squinted at her. "You're lyin'. Kelsey helped us look for you. He wanted to make good with Henry."

Ramona leaned back in the seat. "Ha. He was looking for me because I double-crossed him. After I shot Henry, I told him we'd lay low for a couple of weeks before we got married. But after you sent that note into camp, I knew you were on to me. So I decided to leave with Bull Harmon. Of course, I got rid of him along the way." She shook her head, smiling. "Fools, both of them."

Masters lowered his head. "Just like me."

Ramona sighed. "You're a sucker, Henry. Just like those people who come to fill up your tent."

"I wonder if she's tellin' the truth this time?" Raider said.

"I sure as hell am," Ramona cried. "It was Kelsey all along. He killed the professor and put the gold in his tent. He also planted the gun in his hand. It was easy to convince everyone that the crazy fortune-teller had shot Henry, especially after I made a few turns through camp wearing that stupid cape."

Raider still was not satisfied. "All right, answer me this. Why would Kelsey fake a bump on the noggin and then pretend the gold was stolen from him a second time?"

Ramona shrugged. "A mistake. Harmon was so hot for me that he knocked Jake over the head thinking that he and I would go off together. I had to make it right by making him give the gold back to me. Then I gave Kelsey enough to buy in with Henry. We had planned to kill him anyway and take over the show. It was easier if Jake already owned half of everything."

"She's tellin' the truth," Masters said. "Otherwise why did Kelsey want to get away?"

Raider nodded thoughtfully, rubbing his chin. "Yeah, he did fly in a awful hurry. And he did admit to bein' in love with her. I reckon he's a good enough actor to have made us believe his first story."

Ramona laughed haughtily. "Kelsey was in love with me. Everyone is in love with me."

Henry Masters leaned over in his wife's face. "Not everyone, Ramona. Not anymore."

Her lips curled in a sneer. "You're an old fool, Henry."

He slapped her across the mouth. Hard. She only laughed and spat blood back at him. Raider felt like cuffing her himself, but he didn't think it would be a proper thing to do.

Masters turned away from her. "Tie her up, Raider. We don't want to cheat the hangman." He tossed the piece of rope to the big man.

Ramona's face changed into a frown. "Hangman?"

"That's right," Raider replied. "You'll probably have a noose around your pretty neck, Ramona."

"They'll never hang a woman," she said confidently.

Raider held up the rope for her hands. "I guess you'll just have to take your chances with a judge and jury."

Suddenly she became the helpless Georgia belle. "Please, don't make me ride with my hands tied. I'll go with you. I won't cause any trouble. Just let me get my nosegay. The smell on this train is horrible. My nosegay is in my purse. Here, let me—"

As Ramona Masters leaned over toward her purse, a pistol exploded in the railcar. Her body buckled as the lead tore through her chest. She fell over the seat into her handbag.

Raider wheeled to see the gray-haired man standing at the other end of the car. "Kelsey! How the hell . . ." Cougar Jake held his twin .45s in his hands. Both barrels were smoking.

Kelsey gestured with the Colts. "Move away from her, big man."

Raider glared at the old gunfighter. "You didn't have to do that, Kelsey. She was comin' peaceable."

Cougar Jake nodded toward Ramona's twitching body. "She had a derringer in her purse. Check it if you don't believe me."

Masters looked away from the dying woman, glaring at Kelsey. "Ramona told us some things about you, Cougar. Only we don't know who to believe."

Kelsey smiled. "She told you true, gentlemen. I knew you'd find out sooner or later. That's why I doubled back and caught the train at another station. I knew you'd find her, and I wanted the element of surprise."

Raider's eyes narrowed. "You mean you were behind all of it?"

"I was the one," replied the World's Oldest Living Gunfighter. "But Ramona crossed me. Now, if you'll just step out of the way, I want to get my gold and be gone."

Raider's hand dropped slowly toward his side.

Kelsey thumbed back the hammer of his special-bore Peacemaker. "Don't try it, big man. I'm loaded for bear. I don't want to kill you, but I'll drop you like a bad habit if you force it."

Raider hesitated, wondering if he had a chance against the special loads.

"Drop it," Kelsey urged. "All hardware on the floor."

Raider eased the Colt out of his holster, letting it fall. Kelsey picked up the weapon and threw it to the other end of the car. He then reached back for Ramona's baggage.

"Now," Cougar said, "my money."

Raider's eyes were on the cord for the emergency brake. When Kelsey bent over to pick up the bags, Raider's hand lifted toward the cord. If he could bring things to a screeching halt, maybe he'd have a chance to jump Kelsey and wrestle those pistols away from him.

Kelsey swung back with both barrels pointed at the big man. "Nice try, Arkansas. But no cigar. Move on back that way. And don't let me catch you tryin' anything—Damn it. Damn it . . ."

A small-caliber pistol had sparked behind Cougar Jake. The old man's body buckled with pain. He spun around, staggering a few feet before he fell face down onto his own pistols. Two special loads erupted into his belly. His body trembled in a pool of his own blood.

Raider looked back at the train seat. Ramona Masters was sitting half up with a smoking derringer in her hand. She had shot her former lover and accomplice in the back. Raider wondered if he should reach for his own pistol, but he didn't have to use it after all. The Georgia Nightingale fell backward, dying with a bloody bubble on her lips.

Raider sighed. "I guess she did have a derringer all the time. Just like Kelsey said."

Masters was shaking, not saying a word.

"You all right, Henry?"

The circus promoter wiped the sweat from his forehead. "I could use a drink, my friend. A damned big drink."

Behind them, keys rattled in the door of the car. The conductor stuck his head through, inquiring as to the nature of the damage. "Everyone thinks we're bein' robbed, with all the shooting," he said.

Raider guided Henry toward the conductor. "Take this man back to the mail car. I'll do the rest here."

The conductor gawked at the blood on the floor. "But, these bodies. What should I do?"

"Just take care of Mr. Masters here," Raider replied. "Find him a shot of red-eye. And don't worry about these two. I'll take care of it when we reach Oklahoma City. Go on."

When they were gone, the big man sat down and started to figure out the particulars. He could turn the bodies over to the authorities in Oklahoma City and worry about the report later. Damned paperwork. That was one of the few things Doc had been good for.

Raider also felt that he should accompany Masters back to Kansas City. The promoter might need a hand regrouping his circus. With three of his stars gone, he would have to find replacements. Then, there was always the snake woman and her warm body.

Raider leaned back and slipped off his boots. His feet hurt. They were stinking, too. But somehow the rough-hewn Pinkerton figured that Ramona and Cougar Jake wouldn't mind the smell at all.

EPILOGUE

Raider sat under the big top, perched on the highest seat of the bleachers. He turned the pages of a case report which had been penned for him in Henry Masters's exacting hand. When the circus promoter had asked Raider if there was any way for him to compensate for the return of his gold, the big man had asked him to write the report. Masters had done a good job, much better than Raider would have done himself.

Augie was climbing the bleachers, coming even with the big man just as he had finished reading. "What's it say?"

"Everything," Raider said, frowning. "It makes me sad to think about Ilana. She was a nice woman."

Augie sighed. "I can't believe Kelsey was in on the whole thing all the time. He seemed like a good man."

Raider folded the report and stuck it into an envelope. "Kelsey was a smart one, splittin' off at the last minute so he could keep an eye on us. He was a little late shootin' ole Ramona, though. If he had plugged her sooner, she wouldn't've been able to tell us the truth about him. Course the real mistake was made by Bull Harmon. If he hadn't stole that gold, I never would have been called in. They never woulda staged that bogus deal with the professor, either."

"And Kelsey would have taken over the circus along with Miss Ramona," Augie offered.

"The bad ones always mess up," Raider replied. "And the good ones always seem to get in their way. Ramona tried to play too many spokes against the middle of the wheel. Otherwise she woulda got away with it."

Augie shook his head. "I miss Ilana most of all. I'm sorry she's gone."

"Me too, Augie. Me too." Raider remembered the graves where Kelsey, Bull Harmon, and Ramona Masters were lying. "An eye for an eye. Vengeance belongs to the good Lord."

They turned their eyes back to the center ring. Below them, the Six-gun Circus was once again in rehearsals. Henry Masters had replaced Ilana and Kelsey. They were preparing for the upcoming tour of the Southwest. Raider was going along with them for the first week, just to make sure everything ran smoothly.

Raider noticed Augie's gloomy countenance. "Don't look so sad, Augie. It's over now. Finished. This circus will be on the road in no time. You'll have little kids laughin' at your funny tricks."

Augie put his chin in his hand. "I never wanted to think Ramona was evil. And Mr. Kelsey. How could he do that to his partner? Mr. Masters is such a good man. He'd never hurt anyone."

Raider leaned back. "Don't nobody need a reason to hurt somebody else. Greed has a lot to do with it, but most of the time it's pure meanness."

They watched as the new bareback rider turned another flip.

Raider approved. "She's good. Where'd Henry find her?"

"Paid for her to come all the way from New York," Augie replied. "He can afford it now that you got his money back."

Shots echoed from the corral back to the main tent.

"And the new shootist?" Raider asked.

Augie smiled. "Well, Raider, since you turned down the offer, Mr. Masters just put a notice in the saloons. Now we've got a new Jake Kelsey."

Raider frowned. "You mean Henry's keeping the same name?"

Augie nodded. "It's cheaper and easier than painting over

the new banners. Although he will paint out the Georgia Nightingale."

"Makes sense," Raider replied. "And there ain't no need for ever'one to know about Kelsey's underhanded thievin'. Sorta keeps the legend alive."

Masters stood in the center of the ring barking orders to his people. Once in a while he would look up at Raider and tip his hat. He was not an effusive man, but he planned to thank him later, when the show was well on the road. Until then, he was immersed in his work, trying to forget the pain caused him by his former wife.

Raider tipped his hat to the showman. "He's one hell of a ringmaster."

"Yes," Augie rejoined. "Now if he can just find a tent man to replace Bull Harmon."

"Don't look at me," Raider said. "I ain't workin' on no tent crew."

Augie pleaded with him. "Just for a couple of days. We could use your muscle, Raider."

Raider stood up, winking at the little man. "I'm here to watch out for trouble, Augie, that's an honest day's work. Besides, I got to get this report posted north, so my boss won't worry about me."

Augie pointed a stubby finger at the big man. "You're lazy, that's what you are. Plum lazy!"

"I ain't one to argue," Raider replied. "Especially with the truth."

He started down the bleachers.

"Where are you goin'?" Augie called.

"To the post office."

Augie ran behind him, trying to keep up. "Snakes," the little man cried. "That's where you're going. To the snake lady!"

Raider just kept on walking. He knew Augie was right. And, as the big man had said before, he wasn't one to argue with the truth.

Allan Pinkerton finished the report and handed it to Wagner.

The petulant ramrod of the Pinkerton Agency lifted his

glasses and read in detail the account of the Six-gun Circus case. "Are you sure this is Raider's report?" Wagner asked. "I mean, this appears to have been written by a human being."

Pinkerton frowned. "Why do you dislike him so Wagner?"

"He's brutal. Too quick on the trigger. He believes violence can solve anything. Everywhere he goes, a trail of bodies is left behind."

Pinkerton leaned back in his leather chair, studying his own fingertips in a steeple before his eyes. "You're right, Wagner, of course. Raider is all of those things. That's why I think it's time for me to send him on his way."

Wagner perked up. "You mean you're going to fire him after all?"

Pinkerton lifted another sheaf of papers from the piles on his desk. "No, I'm sending him on another case. Here. Read this."

Wagner protested until his eyes scanned the first few paragraphs of the U.S. territorial marshal's request for assistance.

When he had finished, he looked up at Pinkerton. "We'll never get away from the violence, will we?"

Pinkerton shook his head. "I'll send Raider."

Wagner agreed. The big man from Arkansas was the perfect agent for the assignment.